*Eagles' Wings
to the
Higher Places*

Eagles' Wings
to the
Higher Places

HANNAH HURNARD

Harper & Row, Publishers, San Francisco

Cambridge, Hagerstown, New York, Philadelphia

London, Mexico City, São Paulo, Sydney

1817

FIRST HARPER & ROW EDITION

Designer: Jim Mennick

Library of Congress Cataloging in Publication Data

Hurnard, Hannah
    EAGLES' WINGS TO THE HIGHER PLACES.

    I. Title.
PS3558.U538E2   1981   813'.54   82-48406
ISBN 0-06-064084-7

                86 87 10 9 8 7

Contents

"They that wait upon the Lord shall renew their strength; THEY SHALL MOUNT UP WITH WINGS AS EAGLES; *they shall run, and not be weary; and they shall walk, and not faint."*

Isa. 40:31

Foreword

In 1954, I wrote a book called *Hinds' Feet on High Places* and its sequel, *Mountains of Spices*. This new book, *Eagles' Wings to the Higher Places*, continues the story in the first two books and challenges us to respond to the Highest Ideal which God enables us to see, no matter what the cost. It describes the glorious way in which our capacity to see and respond to higher treasures of Truth contained in the sacred Scriptures is developed, so that new light illumines the pages and we see meanings in its teachings which we were before unable to grasp.

The allegory tells the story of Aletheia (Love of Truth), the daughter of Grace-and-Glory and of Fearless Witness, about whom you may have read in the first books, and how she sets out to follow her parents "farther on and higher up" to the Highest Places of all—the Highest, that is, until "the New Heaven and the New Earth" will be created and "the morning stars will again sing together, and all the sons of God will shout for joy" (Job 38:7) as they behold God bringing into existence still higher and more glorious manifestations of His Love and Goodness.

"I heard the call, 'Come follow!' That was all.
Earth's joys grew dim,
My soul went after Him.
I rose and followed, that was all.
Will you not follow if you hear Him call?"

1

At School in the Low Places

This is the story of Aletheia, the daughter of Grace-and-Glory and Fearless Witness, about whom you may have read in *Hinds' Feet on High Places* and *Mountains of Spices*. Grace-and-Glory and Fearless Witness had lived on the High Places with the King of Love until He called them to work with Him by following Him down to the dark, dark places in the valleys far below, in order to persuade the poor, miserable people who lived there in the darkness to follow them up to the glorious Kingdom of Light and Love on the High Places above.

For a number of years they did this happy though difficult work with the utmost joy in the service of the King whom they both loved so passionately. When to their joy they became the parents of a little daughter, they gave her the beautiful name of Aletheia, which means Love of Truth. While they were down in the valleys with the King of Love, they entrusted her to the tender care of their friends on the High Places, although they returned at intervals to their lovely home on the mountains to be with their little daughter.

Aletheia's early childhood was ideally happy, living on the High Places of God's Love and Truth, playing in the King's Gardens with the other little children of the King's helpers, and experiencing nothing but love and kindness. Each day seemed to shine golden with joy, from the moment that the sun touched the gleaming white peaks of the still Higher Places above them, until the moment those peaks flushed rosy pink with the evening alpine glow and the stars came out one by one, glittering like jewels in the velvety darkness; and it was time to go to bed, ready to wake to another joyful morning after the night's peaceful sleep.

Oh, how the little child Aletheia loved those white, shining peaks towering up heavenwards around her home. Every day she would steal away alone to some quiet spot, look up at them with rapture, and lift her little arms with the passionate longing that they would, by some beautiful enchantment, become wings. Then she could mount up and fly away to the shining heights which, day after day—and even in her dreams—seemed to be beckoning to her and calling to her in a glorious unknown tongue to come to them. She simply could not understand how her mother and father could keep leaving those beautiful gardens on the High Places in order to go down to the dismal, dark valleys so far below. Aletheia herself could hardly bear to look down into those gloomy depths in which it seemed the sun never shone. The valleys were so narrow and hemmed in by steep precipices, such dreary and lonely looking places where surely no one who loved the light and the High Places could bear to live!

Grace-and-Glory knew how much her little daughter loved the distant white peaks towering heavenwards around their home, and told her that they belonged to a yet higher shining world of God's Love and Goodness and Truth. Aletheia herself had been named after them in the hope that she would love the Highest Truth wherever she could see it shining above her, and would always respond to the beckoning call to rise and go "farther on and higher up"; because God is a vast world and universe of Love, reaching far beyond the sky itself, and always calling us to higher and more beautiful glories of truth and love and goodness than can be experienced on the less high levels below.

"Then why do you and Daddy keep going down to the Low Places in those horrid, dark valleys?" asked little Aletheia wonderingly.

Her mother laughed and then said tenderly, "You see, darling, in order to be able to reach and live on these lovely High Places where we are now, your father and I had to live down in those Low Places and gradually develop Hinds' Feet. Then we became able at last to bound up and down these mountain slopes like the wild hinds and gazelles. And that involved quite a long and difficult process, my darling." She was silent and thoughtful for a moment, going back in memory and reliving that whole tremendous experience of developing Hinds' Feet.

"But now we believe the time is soon coming for us to leave these High Places and to rise and go 'farther on and higher up' to those shining ranges of peaks towering up heavenwards beyond us; those heights which you so love to look at and which seem to beckon and call to you with such beautiful voices. But in order to reach those places it is not enough to have Hinds' Feet but Eagles' Wings; and those, my darling little daughter, can only be developed by going down to the dark places in the valleys below to tell the poor people there about these lovely first High Places and to try to persuade them to follow us up here too. This we have been doing, as our Beloved King has told us to do, for a number of years. Now He is telling us that the time has come for us to rise on Eagles' Wings to that shining, still-more-beautiful World of Love above here."

Again she was silent for a moment and then added, with a very special gentleness and tenderness, "Remember, Aletheia, my little daughter, if you too want to be able to rise and reach those beautiful, beckoning heights and join us there, you will have to go down into the dark Low Places and develop, first Hinds' Feet, and then, later on, Eagles' Wings also. And don't be afraid to do it, for the dear King Himself will help you and be with you as He has been with us."

Aletheia never forgot that talk with her mother, for it was one of the last times they were together. One day very soon afterwards, Grace-and-Glory and Fearless Witness called her to them, and, with the utmost love and gentleness, told her that the time had come for them to go on to those Higher Places. It was also the wise and loving will of the King that Aletheia was to go to boarding school down in one of the valleys until she would be old enough to develop Hinds' Feet and Eagles' Wings herself and be able to follow them to that shining world above.

On hearing this news Aletheia began to sob with sorrow and consternation, the first tears she had ever shed. She felt as though her heart would break.

Then she felt her mother's loving arms around her and her voice saying comfortingly, "Darling, you must not be sad, but be glad instead. It is all for the best. If you stayed here, you would not be able to develop even Hinds' Feet, much less Eagles' Wings. Then, one by one, you would find all your friends called away until you were left here quite alone with all the joy and happiness and love departed from your life and no means of escaping and going higher. Go down into the school in the valley, then, as the King bids you do. But, Aletheia, my darling, down there, never, never forget those glorious, shining Higher Places which you have seen. It may be difficult to remember them down there where you will not be able to see them, but keep reminding yourself about them. Remember they are your real home, the Higher Places of Truth and Goodness and Love. You are named 'Love of the Truth' on purpose so that you will constantly be reminded to respond to yet Higher Truths whenever you become able to see them. Then, when your school days come to an end, let nothing hinder you from starting out to reach those shining heights above. Never live or settle down anywhere, my darling, in any place where you cannot see higher heights above you. Always leave such a place and set out to find yet Higher Places and press towards them; for only so will you develop Eagles' Wings and be able at last to reach your real homeland and be with us again."

Then Fearless Witness took his little daughter on his knee and said with the utmost tenderness, and with a great and comforting joy in his voice, "And you must never forget, Aletheia, that whenever you see Higher Places of Truth and Goodness and Love, you must always share what you have seen with others; for if you do not, then the beautiful, beckoning vision will fade, and you will lose it altogether and go no farther. Always keep open to new light, my little daughter, and always share it with others, no matter how difficult and costly it may seem to do so. For light shared brings more light, but light rejected and hidden brings darkness. Never stay behind when the voice of God calls you, for if you do you will find that your summer will end, and all your joys and treasures will wither and fade away, leaving only winter and coldness and terrible loneliness and darkness. But follow the light and rise and join us on the still Higher Places above."

Then they kissed her good-bye and committed her to the love and care of the Great Shepherd of little children, and went their way with the King of Love to the still Higher Places; and Aletheia saw them no more. She had only dimly understood the meaning of what they had said, but their words remained like precious seed sown in her memory, ready to bring forth glorious fruit in due season.

Two of the King's friends took the sorrowful and weaping little girl down to the school in the valley where the King had decreed that she was to spend the next years of her life and left her there.

Oh, how terribly she missed her lovely home on the High Places; the fresh, pure, mountain air; the sound of the streams running merrily through the fields and gardens, singing to themselves as they ran; and the deep, distant roar of the Mighty Waterfall of Love pouring down from the High Places in an ecstasy of self-giving to the Low Places far below, just as her parents had done in their service for the King. But most of all she missed and pined for a glimpse of those shining still Higher Places, the peaks of the Homeland of her heart's desire. Night after night she wept herself to sleep with almost unbearable pangs of homesickness and longing. It seemed to her that she would never know happiness again.

At first, she dreamed of the mountains every night and woke with tears as they faded and were lost to her once again. She felt like a stranger in a foreign country and did not realize that this was really the lovely, rich blessing bequeathed to her by her parents; for she herself was the seed of their passionate love of the High Places of Truth and Goodness, and would never be able to find real satisfaction and joy until she reached them too.

As the years passed she grew more and more unhappy and lonely in the valley, but did not realize why. She no longer dreamt of the mountains and only dimly remembered her golden childhood in the King's Gardens on the High Places. But she never felt at home in the valley, unable to make friends at the school, and became more and more solitary.

Once, when she was about fourteen years old, she

had a very vivid dream which made a lasting impression upon her. She could never forget it, though it filled her with an aching sorrow every time she remembered it. She dreamt that she had wandered away from the school grounds, lonely and miserable as usual, and that she was looking for someone to show her a path or way back to the King's Gardens on the High Places. Then, suddenly, she saw her mother and father leaping and bounding up the rocky, precipitous sides of the valley with the Chief Shepherd Himself. In her dream she saw once again His face, the most beautiful and loving face in the world, looking down at her tenderly and lovingly as she had so often seen Him as a tiny child. With a pang of despair she knew at last what it was she was really longing for and seeking so passionately to find: the Chief Shepherd Himself, to be her Guide and Helper. She stretched out her arms to Him beseechingly, begging Him to take her with Him back to the High Places, but just as she ran towards Him in her dream He vanished, and she found herself back at the gates of the school. A group of girls her own age were standing there talking together in an unusually subdued way. There was a strange look on their faces, and she asked them what had happened. They told her that Someone known as the Great Shepherd had been to the school, had visited with them, and had just left and gone away.

"Left and gone away!" cried Aletheia, feeling as

though her heart would break with pain and longing to
see Him again and to go with Him wherever He might
lead her. "He came while I was away and has left! Oh,
tell me, which way did He go? I must go after Him! I
must, oh, I must find Him!"

The girls looked at her curiously but no one spoke.
Then one of them pointed silently, and Aletheia saw a
little narrow path, hedged in with cruel-looking thorn
trees and strewn with sharp nails and jagged flinty
stones. It led, so it seemed, far, far away, out on to a
wild, rock-strewn hillside. When she saw this, she burst
into a passionate cry of grief and despair and sobbed,
"Did He really go that way—that dreadful way? Oh, I
dare not, I cannot follow after Him along such a path as
that! Oh, oh! I want to go back to the beautiful High
Places where I lived as a little child. I want to follow
Him back there to that beautiful life where everything
was so happy and perfect, not to follow Him along a
cruel path like that. Oh, if only He had stayed here and I
could have begged Him to take me back to the beautiful lost life of the High Places. But He has gone—and I
cannot follow Him all alone along that dreadful path."

Poor Aletheia!—with her passion for the High Places
and her fear and dread of the suffering and difficulties
on the way up to them, just like her mother's fear so
long before. For before they developed Hinds' Feet and
reached the High Places of the Kingdom of Love, both

her parents had been shown the way up there by two great veiled companions—Sorrow and Suffering. Moreover, her parents had both been members of the Fearing Clan down in the Valley of Humiliation, and, before they reached the High Places, her mother's name had been Much Afraid and her father's name Craven Fear; and there was still something of the inherited fear in their daughter, struggling with her passionate longing for the High Places.

Aletheia never forgot that dream and the bitter, poignant despair that had filled her heart on discovering that the Great Shepherd had actually been there while she was away. She had lost the chance to follow Him because of her dread of the thorn-and-nail strewn path along which he had gone.

After that she dreamed no more of the High Places nor of her childhood home—and she grew lonelier than ever.

2
The Mountain Top City

Several years dragged by until it was nearly time for Aletheia to leave the school and start a new kind of life, though she had no idea what she would do.

Then something quite unexpected happened. One of her classmates named Evangelica invited her to spend the last school holiday with her family, who lived in a place called Mountain Top City.

This was something completely new, for Aletheia had been accustomed to spend the holidays drearily with strangers, wherever the principal of the school could find someone willing to take in the lonely child. None of her schoolmates had ever invited her, for she was so dreary and solitary that they felt uncomfortable in her presence, especially as she never seemed to want to be in their company. On this occasion, too, she would certainly have been unwilling to accept her schoolmate's invitation, for she had grown so shy and awkward she dreaded being with strangers. But there was something about the name Mountain Top City which quickened her pulse and stirred a longing excitement in her heart. Oh, how wonderful to be among mountains again at long last, and even on a mountain top. Perhaps from there she would be able to catch a glimpse of her long lost, beloved home on the High Places of Love. She felt she simply must go, so shyly and awkwardly she accepted the invitation.

Sure enough, the train they travelled in did bring them at last to the foot of a beautiful mountain, its lower slopes covered with peaceful, green pastures and pine woods, towering higher up into steep, rocky cliffs. A little funicular railway took them both up the mountainside, and at the top her friend's parents and brother were waiting to meet them. They greeted Aletheia very kindly indeed and made her welcome.

The city itself lay foursquare and was completely surrounded by high walls with many turrets. It enclosed a very large area, for within the walls there were beautiful gardens, vineyards, and parks, as well as dwelling places and buildings of many kinds, especially churches with wonderful spires pointing heavenwards and many other places of worship.

Evangelica's parents owned a large, handsome house surrounded by a big garden. How Aletheia revelled in the fresh pure air of the mountain top, and how amazingly quickly she entered into the life of the family who so lovingly initiated her into their ways, pleasures, and interests. But best of all they were actually able to teach her once again many of the things she had known dimly as a little child on the High Places, but had long since forgotten. The loveliest thing they did for her was to remind her that though she could not visibly see the Great Shepherd she had known and loved as a little child, she could speak to Him whenever she wished to do so, for He was always close at hand; and she learned daily, little by little but quite clearly, to hear Him speaking back to her and to recognize His voice. Oh, how is it possible to describe Aletheia's joy and delight as once again she truly began to experience the presence of the Good Shepherd and to hear His loving voice guiding, encouraging, and strengthening her. The times of communion with Him alone in the early mornings here in Mountain Top City made Aletheia feel as though she had actually been born again, that she was beginning a completely new and wonderful life full of joys she had never believed could be possible when she was down in the dark valley. The love and gratitude which she felt towards her new friends cannot be expressed in words. It was as though she had found new parents and need never feel orphaned and lonely again.

Indeed, she became so much at home with them and responded so gratefully and joyfully to all that they could teach her, that they lovingly invited her to return and live with them as soon as the last term at school ended; to become a second daughter to them and a sister to Evangelica and her brother Zeal; and to join them in their work in Mountain Top City. This she joyfully did.

And what was the work in which they were all so busily engaged in Mountain Top City? It consisted in earnest, devoted efforts to persuade other people to come and live with them up there, too. For outside the walls of their city, on the mountain slopes, there were many little villages and other quite large towns. From the top of the walls of their own city it was possible to see to far distances, and down into deep valleys below. Everywhere one looked, there were these other places filled with people going busily about their own affairs. Down in the valleys, people were doing dark, dismal, and often dreadful things. Indeed, their lives were very unhappy because they lived so far below with little or no light. They knew nothing about the beautiful and blessed life in Mountain Top City. But even people living higher up the mountainside—indeed some of them nearly on the mountain top itself—were in a very bad way, too. Their lives were almost worse than those far down in the dark valleys, because they supposed that living on the mountain slopes meant that they were living in the true light, and needed nothing more. Only those privileged to live in Mountain Top City itself, however, knew and experienced the only real life which could make it possible for them to enter into endless life and blessedness in a higher world after death. Everyone else, without exception, lived in darkness and ignorance; unless they could be persuaded to come right up to the top of the mountain and live in the beautiful city there, they would, perforce, spend all their lives in darkness. They would die without knowing the truth. They would miss their chance forever, because after death they would enter into endless darkness, woe, and anguish, since they had not loved and chosen the light and had refused to leave everything in the Lower Places and live the blessed life in Mountain Top City.

Her new family explained this most earnestly and lovingly to Aletheia; they urged her to realize that the one great work incumbent upon them all was to warn people and entreat them to leave the dark places below while they still had the chance to do so. She gladly entered one of their Training Institutes in company with Evangelica and Zeal in order to learn how best to devote her life to this supremely important work. She was very happy to do this, for she longed to share the new joy and blessing she was experiencing with everyone she met, especially with the people in the low, dark valleys where she had been so miserable herself. For why should she be privileged to be delivered from the dark places and to live in Mountain Top City, while multitudes still toiled in the darkness and often suffered all their life long, dying with no hope of finding the light anywhere? Aletheia shivered at the thought. Why must they go on suffering and living in the darkness for ever and ever?

It was certainly very urgent that all who knew the truth do everything in their power to share the Good News concerning a blessed Higher Life and the very Bad News for all who rejected the invitation that they must forever lose the opportunity of leaving the darkness and suffer in a self-made hell with evildoers, tormenting each other forever. The realization of this truth made Aletheia and her friends Evangelica and Zeal earnestly devote their lives to spreading the Good and Bad News wherever they went, so that they would never have to reproach themselves with the thought that they had selfishly and indifferently left people unwarned or ignorant of the King's invitation.

In this earnest ministry of theirs they grew so close together that soon, added to the joy of her new life on the mountain top, Aletheia found that she and Zeal were one in their supreme desire to spread the Good and Dreadful News. It was evident, both to themselves and to all their friends, that they should be joined in a still closer bond. They became engaged to be married, to the great joy of Evangelica and her parents, who delighted in the zeal with which the two young people witnessed. For what could be more suitable and blessed than a union between Love of Truth and Zeal in witness to the truth! So thought everyone, and Aletheia's adopted parents rejoiced especially that the unhappy young girl they had rescued from the Low Places should now become a real member of the family.

Strangely enough, after a time Aletheia began to experience a vague but very deep unrest or uneasiness; this grew stronger each day that passed and tinged all her happiness with something like unhappiness, though that was not the right name, she felt, by which to describe it. She could not understand it, and it left her puzzled and distressed. At first she told herself that it was her sincere grief over the hopeless condition of the people down in the dark places where she and her young companions visited, either in pairs or in groups, holding open-air meetings and pleading with the people to come and live in Mountain Top City; and the complete unwillingness of anyone to respond to the wonderfully Good News from the King of Love, inviting them to enter His Kingdom and be happy and blessed forever. They were equally unresponsive to the very Bad News which warned them that if they rejected this invitation they must suffer forever with no hope of a further opportunity to repent.

It was the custom of the young people in the Training Institute in Mountain Top City to go out in groups or two by two, visiting from house to house in the villages outside the city, pleading with the people to listen to the message. Over and over again doors would be slammed in their faces, and when they stood pleading in the open air, the streets of the village or town would be empty or have only one or two passersby who stared curiously but showed no intention of stopping more than a moment to listen. Each week, also, it was their custom to broadcast the same Good and Bad News through loudspeakers placed in the turrets on the city walls, so that the message might go forth far and wide over the mountainside and be heard everywhere. But there was very little, if any, result.

Loudspeakers proclaiming various different messages were also heard broadcasting from towns and places on the mountainside. As soon as the sound of those alien broadcasts were heard in Mountain Top City, everyone was warned not to listen because those messages came from the Lower Places and contained dangerous and misleading errors. They could all too easily lead one into great danger, and even beguile one into leaving the truth and safety of Mountain Top City itself to go live in the "worldly" Lower Places outside. So Aletheia and her friends never for a moment paused to listen to what was being broadcast in that way. It did occur to her that the people in all those other villages and towns were all too obviously treating their own earnest and passionately entreating broadcast messages in the same way.

It is no wonder, then, that at first she told herself that the sorrowful unrest deep in her heart was caused by the hopeless condition of those she so greatly longed to rescue and save. For it generally came when she lay awake in the night after a busy day out witnessing in the villages. Even more, it happened in the very early mornings when, according to the blessed habit which her mountain top friends had taught her, she went up on to the walls of the city to commune alone with the King whose visible Presence she could not see, but whose Voice she heard speaking to her so lovingly in her heart.

As the days passed, it became more than a vague unrest and began to pierce her heart with a poignant, painful longing for something which she could not name.

Then at last, one morning very early indeed, when she was keeping her tryst up on the city wall, light broke into her understanding. She knew what the painful, poignant unrest was really rooted in. It was the old passionate longing for the still Higher Places which she had seen from her childhood's first home. Once again she seemed to hear her mother's gentle, loving voice saying, "Aletheia, my darling, if ever you find yourself living in any place from which you cannot see any still

Higher Places of God's Goodness and Love, don't stay there but get up and seek until you can see them."

Yes, that was it, though she had never realized it before. But from the beautiful Mountain Top City where she was living there were no Higher Places to be seen anywhere, for were they not the privileged few people who had arrived on the mountain top itself? *All* the truth was theirs; all they had to do was to live it and witness it and press it upon others. So there were no beautiful, white peaks gleaming heavenwards there, calling and beckoning with promises of still lovelier revelations of the Nature of the Eternally Higher Goodness of the Highest of All.

Then like great waves and billows the homesick longing for the Higher Places broke over Aletheia's soul. She felt like an orphan child again, even up here on Mountain Top City, just as she had felt when she was first led down to the school in the Low Places. To the depths of her soul she knew that she could live here no longer where there were no Higher Places in sight. No, it was not sorrow for the hopeless plight of the poor people in the dark places which caused her grief; it was anguish at the thought of the hopelessness of the only message which she had to give them. Lost forever with no hope if they rejected it! Cast off by the God who had brought them into existence, if they rejected His call now. All her unacknowledged doubts and questions arose again concerning a God who called Himself Love and who brought myriads of souls into existence without being able to prevent them from condemning themselves to an eternity of hopeless darkness and suffering, lost to Him forever. How could He possibly love them, if He let this happen to them? How could He possibly be good, if He brought them into an existence where it was possible for them to separate themselves from His love and joy and goodness forever?

Of course, the answer to such a question was that He had gone to all possible lengths in seeking to save them and restore them to Himself—even going to the cross, carrying their sins, and offering them forgiveness. But if this was rejected He could do no more. "He is a *holy* God," she had been taught, and if His creatures choose to love evil more than good, they cannot dwell in His Presence. They have only themselves to blame, even if they were born into situations where they were surrounded by evil influences and led into evil desires. But, Oh, cried Aletheia's heart in an agony of despair, Oh, how terrible and hopeless to be a God who loves goodness and cannot save His own creatures from preferring evil. If he did not call Himself a God of Love it would be different. A devil might create living souls capable of tormenting themselves forever. Oh, what agony to love the souls brought into existence enough to go to the cross in a last supreme effort to save them and not be able to do so. To proclaim, "I, if I be lifted up, will draw *all* men unto Myself," and to be unable to do it! To find that the Devil is stronger than Goodness and could gloatingly and triumphantly succeed in damning at least ninety percent of God's creatures, leaving only a pitiful ten or even smaller percent to respond to His love—a handful of souls for Him to rejoice over for ever and ever, while all the others were tormented in hell. Oh, what hopelessly bitter Bad News this was. How could she ever believe in and trust such a God again?

Then suddenly Aletheia remembered her parents and the joy on their faces each time they bade her farewell in order to go down into the Low Places with the King of Love to proclaim what they called the best possible Good News. Why, their faces had been like shining reflections of the joy and love and triumph in His own face! They had gone with the King down into the Hells of the Low Places in order to help people out of them, not to tell them why they were in danger of endlessly staying there.

"Oh, for the High Places and the still Higher Places!" cried Aletheia in anguish of spirit. Somewhere Higher from where I can see *more* of God's goodness and love and understand the real truth which made my parents and the King so happy. What was the message which they took with them down into the valleys? Surely, oh surely there must be better News than I have learnt about here in Mountain Top City!

Then all these doubts and anguished questions seemed to crystallize and express themselves in the words of a poor, tormented man whom she had recently spoken to down in one of the lowest places of all. He had opened the door in answer to her knock and she had begun to tell him about the very good and the very dreadful news which she was commissioned to bring him. His only repsonse had been to exclaim with an oath, "Don't talk to me about a God of Love who rejects us poor wretches forever because we can't help choosing and doing evil. I'd rather stay like this than be with someone who permits endless hells. If He made us and loves us why doesn't He come and share the hells He lets us make for ourselves. We might believe in Him and His so-called love and grace if He did that instead of just looking on from a throne far off in heaven. What is the use of sending someone to die for our sins on a cross two thousand years ago and then leaving us in our sins? Let Him come down into Hell with us and see if He can rescue us out of it!"

The words the poor, desperate man had flung at her rang again in Aletheia's ears. "If He made us and really loves us let Him come and deliver us from Hell forever!"

"Why doesn't He?" cried the voice in her soul in an

agony of bewilderment and sorrow. Then a still, small voice answered in the words of one who had plumbed the depths of despair and hopelessness and had found the answer.

"Though I make my bed in hell, EVEN THERE THOU ART WITH ME" (Ps. 139:8).

Aletheia sprang to her feet. She looked yearningly in every direction. "O King of Love," she cried. "Where are the high peaks of your love and goodness? Show me, oh, show me the way to the lost Higher Places!"

She strained her eyes, searching longingly in every direction, and expecting to see far, far away somewhere, the white shining peaks she had so loved as a little child. But no! It *was* true. This was Mountain Top City, and there were no Higher Places to be seen in any direction. The wall and turret on which she was standing was the highest place anywhere within sight.

Well, no—not quite the highest place. For there, eastward, outside the city wall, there was a great rampart of dark, jagged rocks, and the summits of those rocks *were* a little higher than the city walls; indeed, they entirely blocked the view eastward. That was why the main gates of the city were in the western wall, and not one gate on the eastern side. For who would want to look out—much less go out—on to the barren desert which terminated in that dark, rocky barrier.

"Never stay anywhere where you cannot see Higher

Places, my darling." Again her mother's words rang in her ears, and on a sudden impulse, Aletheia went down the turret steps and hurried along the eastern wall, looking for a place where she could descend to the desert outside. She came presently to a steep, stone staircase, ruined and crumbling in some places through long disuse and lack of repair, which led her down to the stony desert outside the city. Panting, her hands scratched and her dress torn from her scramble down the steps, she turned and hurried towards the grim rock barrier and began to climb up towards the highest crag that she could see; then she came to the summit.

Standing there on a flat rock, she lifted her arms heavenwards, as she had so often done as a little child, longing for them to become wings, and looked up. Just as the sun rose and flushed them rosy pink far, far away eastwards and towering heavenwards in glorious splendor, she saw the range and peaks of the Higher Places, and burst into tears of joy.

"The High Places!" she cried. "My Homeland! And beyond them the still Higher Places. O God, thank You! Thank You! Show me the way to them, I beseech You. It is time for me to start on my journey to the Higher Places—to my real Homeland."

3

The
Abyss
of Love

The sound as of a great door opening behind her caused Aletheia to look around. Like the covers of a great book, a door in the rocks swung open. Standing in the door as though he were turning her to the first page of the book, was a man whose face shone with love and kindness.

"Aletheia, come here," he said, and it was as though heaven itself were welcoming her. "Come with me, and I will show you the path that leads to those shining High Places you so long to reach. Come and behold a vision of a yet higher Truth than you have been able to see before, on your journey to full God-consciousness."

He held out both hands as he spoke and with a glad cry Aletheia sprang down the rocks and stood beside him. It seemed to her that until that moment she had never known what real happiness was. Here at last was someone who could show her the way to the Higher Places of her heart's desire. As she looked into his face she could not possibly doubt him, for the very name of the Good Shepherd and King of Love was beautifully inscribed upon his forehead; and the light that shone out of his eyes was the Light of the Kingdom of Love itself.

He took her hand, saying gently, "God is an infinite ocean of Love and Goodness. In Him there is no wrath at all. What men call His wrath and judgment is the inexorable determination of the love of the skilled surgeon to heal the sickness and suffering of a beloved son, no matter at what cost to Himself and to the son, so that no trace of anything that can hurt or harm the beloved one remains. I will lead you to a place where you will behold the higher truth which will solve completely all your sorrowful questioning."

So saying, he led her through the doorway of the first page of the great book, and it closed behind them. To Aletheia it seemed as though she had entered another world altogether. It was a quiet, wooded place, apparently on the outskirts of a large forest. The sun shone brightly, and the sky was blue. In the distance they could hear the sound of the hooves of a horse cantering towards them along a little bridlepath and the merry jingling of bells. Almost at once the horse and its rider came in sight. A richly dressed young man with a plumed hat was riding a gaily caparisoned chestnut-red horse. Just before reaching the place where they stood, the horse began rearing and plunging as though in fear. A most deplorable figure had stepped out from the shade of the forest trees and now stood in the middle of the bridlepath. It was the figure of an almost naked man, his body covered with leprous sores. Nose, eyelids, and lips had been eaten away by the frightful disease, leaving only holes in his face. He was holding up the pitiful stumps of two hands from which all the fingers had been well-nigh eaten, and from the hole of his mouth there came a woeful, entreating, but wordless cry.

Aletheia shrank back in horror. She had never conceived of such suffering. The gaily dressed rider on the plunging horse dug his spurs into its flanks as though to urge it away from the dreadful sight and from the polluted air as soon as possible, while at the same time he flung his purse towards the poor, beseeching figure. But at that very moment a burning shaft of white light shone down from heaven, as though an Angel stood behind the leprous beggar, enfolding him in his wings. In the blazing beam of that light Aletheia saw that the young rider had checked his horse and, springing from its back, was running towards the leper. Then kneeling beside him on the ground, he was lifting the pitiful stumps of hands to his lips and kissing them, tears streaming down his cheeks, and exclaiming in horrified distress and shame:

"O my Lord and my God, is it indeed in this form that You come to me? Is it true that You who created all things also inhabit all things by Your Spirit? That You, the transcendent God, are also immanent in every part of Your creation, even though it is now a fallen one, feeling what all the creatures feel from the greatest to the least! That 'In all their afflictions You are afflicted, and the Angel of Your Presence with and in them saves them' (Isa. 63:9)? That in this desolate, leprous beggar You come to me and ask for my love and help in seeking to alleviate the afflictions which You Yourself are sharing with him? Here I am, O my Lord and my God! For the rest of my life I am Yours alone, to be shown by You how to pour out loving service to all Your creatures in distress and need. For now I see that the answer to all my prayers is to be shown how to spend my life in the glory of God, and the only way by which I can express my love to You, my Creator and Lord, is by expressing it to You as You suffer in your fallen creatures. What I do to them, I do also to You. O my Lord and my God, I have truly found You at last and fall at Your feet and offer my life to You. As long as you are crucified in Your fallen suffering creatures I have only one thing to do: to love and serve You by loving and serving them."

Aletheia could not be sure whether these words were spoken by the young man kneeling beside the leper, by the loving guide whose hand she was holding, or by her own awed and trembling heart. All she knew was that a veil had been rent from top to bottom, revealing a long-hidden mystery almost too great to be taken in: the vision of a God unutterably greater and more glorious in grace, love, compassionate tenderness, and inexorable determination to save and rescue *all* His creatures than anything she had heard or been shown about Him before.

The white burning light and her stinging tears caused her to close her eyes for a moment. When she looked again, the forest, the leper, the rider, and his horse had all vanished, and she and her guide were standing on the very edge of a vast, bottomless abyss with mighty, canyonlike, rocky walls. As the tear mist vanished from her eyes, she saw that, lying from one end to the other of that vast canyon, there stretched a mighty, well-nigh unending cross, with a living Body nailed to it in terrible anguish. Then she heard her guide's voice saying gently, "That Body, pierced by nails to this cross of anguish, is the whole Body of Fallen Mankind, nailed there by their sins and selfish cruelty towards each other, and even more by their cruel neglect of the sufferings of each other. For the Great Law is that what we do to others we do to ourselves also, and by our sins we all crucify ourselves to this cross of disease and sickness, woe, want, hunger, loneliness, torturing pain, and lingering death. All the ages of Men—from the beginning of time to the end—are there; and all Mankind together—men, women, and little children—in the eyes of God form only One Body—the body of His fallen, self-crucified Son, Adam the First, 'the Son of God' (Luke 3:38). That is the meaning of the cross once raised up 'in Time' two thousand years ago. That fallen Man is a crucified Mankind, nailed to a cross of unutterable woe from which the Great Father is determined, no matter at what cost to Himself and to mankind, to rescue them for ever and ever. In a moment you will see how He does this. But first look. What do you see there in that nearest foot of the nail-pierced body?"

Shuddering and dismayed, Aletheia looked; and there amongst the other quivering, tortured cells in the foot she saw the desolate leper and the youth kneeling beside him, on the edge of the forest they had just left. The bloodstream flowing through the breadth of that tortured Body flowed over and into the hands of the young man, Francis of Assisi, and thence into the leprous body with healing power. Yes, everywhere in that Body the tortured cells were being healed one after another by the bloodstream flowing into partially-healed cells and from them into those which were still suffering so fearfully.

"God sees us all as One Man," whispered Aletheia to herself through trembling lips. "All of us are cells in the *One* body of Fallen Mankind."

"Look further, Aletheia," said the voice of her guide. "There is still more for you to see. Raise your eyes and look towards the head of the Body and at the *face* that you will see there—the face of the One Being Who is conscious in the whole Body and feels and experiences what every single cell in the Body is experiencing. Look and behold the amazing, unsearchable, and incomprehensible Love of God."

"I can't—I can't look!" faltered Aletheia. "I cannot bear to look upon the awful suffering which must be stamped upon the countenance of the One who feels it all!"

"Only look," urged her guide. "Are you not longing for the Truth? Look and see it!"

Slowly, shuddering with almost unbearable dread, Aletheia let her eyes travel shrinkingly all along that suffering Body until she could see the shoulders, the neck, and then—almost blinded by tears—the face of that crucified Being.

What she saw transfixed her, for it was the face of the King of Love Himself—the Good Shepherd—"laying down His own Life for the Sheep." It was His Blood coursing through the whole, tortured Body which was carrying life and healing to all the cells. Yes, it was the face of Love Himself, the Divine, Eternal Love of the

God Who is not only transcendent and fills all the eternities, but Who also has become immanent in His own Creation. Two thousand years ago the stupendous truth was revealed for all to see by the One who hung nailed to a cross of anguish between two thieves and murderers, sharing with them the horror of the hells which they had made for themselves.

It was the expression on the face of that crucified Being which filled Aletheia with adoring wonder, awe, and joy, for that face shone with unutterable joy and triumphant love; and the joy blotted out every trace of anguish. It was indeed the face of One Who "for the joy set before Him, endured the cross, despising the shame" and exulted in the ultimate victory. It was so marvelous and glorious, that Aletheia felt that her heart must burst with the rapture of it.

For lo, rising up behind the crucified Body, just where the head lay, was another glorious resurrection Body. It was not stretched from one end of the canyon to the other, but rose upright, higher and higher into the very highest heavens themselves—a shining, white, glorified Body purged of every spot, wrinkle, and stain, burning with Heavenly power, glory, and splendor. That resurrection Body grew (even as she looked at it) greater and more glorious, for it was composed of all the cells in the Body on the cross which had passed through the purging anguish of the hells of suffering on the cross. Thus, the cells were healed, purified, and purged from all evil. Finally, they were carried in the bloodstream closer and closer to the head of the Body—the face of their Divine Lover and Saviour—and then drawn up from the Body of Death into the glorious Body of His Resurrection.

Aletheia could see the body on the cross of anguish dwindling and shrinking into death, literally disintegrating as the healed cells carried by the bloodstream were brought to the head of the body and to the place of Resurrection. The Body of Resurrection, as the crucified One shrivelled and dwindled, grew greater, stronger, and mightier all the time, as the healed cells were added to it. In the end—there could be no doubt of it—there would be nothing left on the cross—not even a dead body, for all was being swallowed up in life and victory.

"He is the Saviour of *all* men!" (1 Tim. 4:10). The words burst forth in passionate triumph from the lips of Aletheia. "Oh, how blind I have been! He is lifted up and nailed to the cross with us. As Jesus revealed when He hung between the two thieves and murderers, He *will* 'draw *all* men unto Him.'

" 'As in Adam (poor fallen Mankind) all die, so in Christ, the Second Adam, shall *all* men be made alive' (1 Cor. 15:22). Oh, what a victory! The only victory truly worthy of the Great God and Creator Who 'did not make anything in vain but in the end restores *all* things unto Himself' (Acts 3:21). Oh, it is the Best News possible, the only possible News, if we are truly to love and trust Him fully. Oh, what terribly Bad News I have been trying to pass off as Good News. When I look upon this, I see that it is the only possible meaning in the Revelation given by the Good Shepherd when He was here on earth and laid down His life on the cross in order to show us the Truth and to reveal the Father as He really is."

> What grace! our sins borne and forgiven!
> What Love! our sufferings shared as well!
> God leads us to His Highest heaven:
> Comes to us in our deepest hell!
> Here at the Cross alone we find
> His saving power for ALL MANKIND.

Then she heard a voice speaking from the cross, issuing from the lips of the All-Conquering Savior.

"You who are able to behold these things are My witnesses. You must share this Truth with others. Behold, I ordain you and send you forth to proclaim this glorious News. Remember, you must share what you have seen or the vision will fade from your soul and the darkest night of all descend upon it—until the final daybreak and the shadows flee away. Tell everyone that whatever you do to any member in the one great Body of Mankind, you do to yourself too and *you do it unto Me.*"

Then the veil of mist spread once again over the fathomless Abyss of Love. The cross and the Body upon it vanished from Aletheia's sight, and she found that she was sitting alone on the rocky barrier and behind her lay Mountain Top City. It was dark. The sun had gone down, and the light had faded. Aletheia knew that, for her, there would never be real light in the city again, only a dim candlelight in contrast to the glory she had seen.

4

The Leap over the Wall

Aletheia slowly felt her way back to the eastern wall of the city, and as she went, the words rang in her ears like a clarion call: "You are my witnesses. You who have seen this Truth must show it to others, too." Her father's words also came back to her. "Aletheia, you must always bear witness to any new and higher truth you see. For light shared brings more light. But light rejected or hidden brings darkness."

As she groped her way to the little staircase on the eastern wall, Aletheia suddenly shivered and found that she was trembling. She began to feel a reaction following the exultation which had filled her heart on the edge of the Abyss of Love. She felt that the hour of a great crisis and choice was now upon her—to tell or not to tell about the glory that had been shown her and to so many others, too, but to no one in Mountain Top City! To do so, she knew, would mean utter rejection by those who had not seen the same vision and who sincerely believed that *all* the truth had been entrusted to those who dwelt in the city. How could she possibly tell her beloved adopted parents to whom she owed so much? She realized only too well that it would break their hearts, and that it would mean that she could no longer live and work with them in Mountain Top City. Indeed, how could she explain that she herself now knew it was only one stage on a long and glorious ascent to Higher Places of Truth and Love? She felt that she had seen a completely new God to love and worship, so much higher and more glorious was her understanding now of His nature, love, and power than what she had learnt about Him from her beloved teachers in the city.

The more she pictured to herself what would happen if she sought to share the new, glorious understanding which had been given her, the more her heart sank. She trembled at the very thought of telling her beloved friends that she could no longer witness with them unless she could proclaim the only truly Good News about the King of Love which was worthy of His Victory and Grace. She knew that they would say, sorrowfully and with the strongest possible warnings, that she had allowed herself to be snared into believing dangerous error that absolutely contradicted the teachings contained in the One Infallible Book of Truth.

The extraordinary thing was that the more Aletheia pondered on the vision of the Abyss of Love, the more crystal clear it became to her. Everything in the Beloved Book of Truth proclaimed and confirmed that what she had seen was true and the only possible meaning of the revelation of God's love and grace portrayed therein. Moreover, it gave the only possible explanation worthy of a God of Love, as well as to all the dark and mysterious passages and sayings in the Book which had caused her such anxious and troubled questionings. It did not contradict the Book at all, but only opened up its true meaning in the most marvelous way. However, it certainly did contradict some of the most "Fundamental Doctrines" and interpretations of its Scriptures that were dearest to the hearts of the dwellers in Mountain Top City.

How could she possibly tell her friends and companions in the work that she could no longer share in proclaiming their Good News, as they and she and Zeal had so earnestly done in the past? It now seemed to her to be the most dreadful News possible, because it left Evil and the devil so evidently much stronger than Goodness and God Himself. All their missionary zeal had been motivated by the desire to warn people of endless hells and separation from God's Presence; but, oh, how dreadful to think that once they drew their last breath and died, God Himself could do no more to rescue them and the devil would gloat forever that he had been so successful in persuading such vast multitudes to damn themselves hopelessly to the darkness and torment he had lured them into.

Above all, what would Zeal—her most beloved friend of all—say when she told him of these things? There could be little doubt that this must be the end of their friendship and the crucifixion of their love. Zeal, more than all her other companions in the city, was the most zealous and devoted in warning others about the danger of being lost in an endless hell if they did not believe and respond to the message.

Kneeling alone in her room, Aletheia found her soul swept by tempests of temptation to remain silent and not to jeopardize the happy and blessed fellowship of her life in Mountain Top City. After all, why should she not keep the glorious thing which she had seen a hidden treasure in her own heart and rejoice in it? Why not wait until in some wonderful way God Himself, in His own time, helped her friends to see it too, just as He had so graciously led her to see it?

But deeply imprinted in her soul was the memory of that face into which she had looked—the face of the suffering love of God Himself sharing the Cross with all His creatures. How could she continue to preach a Gospel that described His love and mercy in such a way that multitudes who heard about it turned away, com-

pletely unattracted or even repelled by a concept of a
God so different from the One she had seen revealed in
the Abyss of Love? If only they could see Him as she
had, even the most hardened and careless souls would
assuredly, in the end, come to Him in thankful adoring
love—as to the One true Lover of their souls from
whose love nothing in life and death, in sorrow or tribu-
lation, or in hell itself could possibly separate them.

Again and again the words rang in her ears: "You
who have seen these things are My witnesses. Behold, I
ordain you and send you forth to proclaim the glorious
News." And again, "I, if I be lifted up as the truth which
you have seen about the suffering Love of God, sharing
all the afflictions of His creatures with them until they
are drawn to respond to His love—I will draw all men
to Myself" (John 12:32).

"Yes, my Lord," whispered Aletheia through trembling lips and from a trembling heart. "By Your grace *I
will* do it, and You will give me the power to do it."

When it was her turn to speak once again through
the loudspeaker to the people outside the city, she explained to her friends that she could not do so unless
she were allowed to share an infinitely more wonderful
Gospel of grace and salvation than she had known
about before. She told them of her experience on the
edge of the Abyss of Love.

The horrified reactions of her friends to this news

and to the higher truth she sought to share with them
was even greater than anything she had expected or
imagined; it caused not only the utmost distress and
consternation, but from many quarters, also, the strongest possible condemnation. The news ran like wildfire
through the city, and she was told that she could have
no further share of any kind in their work and witness.
Henceforth, she must be an outsider and every opportunity to work with them for the King was closed.

Naturally, it was the sorrow and distress of her beloved adopted parents and brother and sister which
Aletheia found hardest to bear. To see their heartbroken sorrow as they discovered that "all their labor and
love bestowed upon her" had been in vain, and that she
had actually become a traitor in their midst, caused
such anguish of heart to Aletheia that she did not know
how she could bear it.

As for Zeal, he said little at first, but the expression
of heartbroken horror on his face was like a knife in her
own heart. He kept apart as much as possible until
everyone else had had their say, and then he came to her
and pleaded with her passionately to give up the whole
idea of trying to witness to the new and dreadful error
in which she had become entangled. "For the sake of all
those young people who have been helped by you in
this city, Aletheia," he pleaded, "say no more of this
matter. Think how many young believers led to our

Lord, through your witness, will now stumble and probably be shaken in their faith. For their sakes confess that you realize that you have been led into error and are thankful to be shown this by those far older in the faith and in the spiritual life than you are. Come back to us, Aletheia, my darling, and we will forget this dreadful happening. We will go forward together in the happy life of witness in which we plan to be joined to our life's end. For the sake of so many believers—and for my sake, who must give you up if you persist in this error—come back to us, repent, and be restored."

Aletheia raised her sorrowful eyes to his face and said with heartbroken love, "Zeal, my most beloved friend and companion, you speak like an angel of light, but, alas, I know that it is the tempter seeking to turn me back. Zeal, listen to me. I CANNOT UNSEE WHAT I HAVE SEEN: I CANNOT UNLOVE THE HIGHEST LOVE OF ALL, into Whose face I have looked—nailed there on the cross in the Body of suffering fallen Mankind. You of all human beings, I love most dearly and truly, but there is one thing that I love even more: the Truth that I have seen. Even for your sake, Zeal, I cannot keep silent; and I cannot go back to witnessing to something, which now seems to me to be so much less than the full Truth that it is almost like a distortion of it. No, I must rise and go further on and Higher Up towards the still Higher Places of revelation and love."

So Mountain Top City was closed to Aletheia. That night she went out from her adopted home for the last time and, weeping silently with a broken heart, made her way to the top of the eastern wall.

For a while she stood silently up there looking out at the twinkling lights of the city where, after years of sorrow and loneliness, she had found such happiness and so much blessing. Now she must lay it all down into the darkness of loss and separation. How dark the night felt around her! Then some words sprang to her lips from one of the songs in the beloved Book of Truth. "Thou, O Lord, wilt light my candle; the Lord my God will enlighten my darkness. It is God which girdeth me with strength, and maketh my way perfect. He maketh my feet like hinds' feet and setteth me upon high places" (Ps. 18:28, 32, 33).

These were the words that had been so precious to her mother when she was still Much Afraid and only just starting to the High Places. Aletheia gave a little sob of sorrow and a little laugh of joy and said, "What You did for my mother, You will do for me, my Lord. I *will* go outside the camp with You, bearing Your reproach. Here I am."

Then turning away from the twinkling lights in the homes of her friends in the city, she began to make her way down the crumbling steps of the little stone stairway. But before she reached the bottom, she found that the stairway had either crumbled away completely or had been deliberately broken off, perhaps so that no one else would try to make the dangerous and erroneous attempt to reach the rocky barrier eastwards outside the city. The steps broke off completely several feet above the rocky ground below. There was nothing else to do, unless she turned back, except jump.

She leapt from the last step to the ground below and landed in a little heap on the stones and sand. She was bruised and slightly cut and bleeding, but suffered no real damage.

As she slowly struggled to her feet, an amazing thing happened. A flood of joy surged through her heart like a bubbling river, and she found herself laughing aloud. "I'm free! I'm outside! Nothing can bind me again. By Thee, O Lord, I have run through a troop; by Thee I have leaped over a wall" (Ps. 18:29).

"Leaped over a wall!" she repeated, and laughed again. "No, not exactly leaped over the wall, but scrabbled over it and fallen in a heap! But oh, I am outside the wall. I am really free! No one can ever tell me again what I may, and what I may not, believe, but You, My Lord; and You are the Truth itself revealing Yourself to me."

Then looking around in the darkness, she spied a tiny, twinkling light. Making her way toward it, she came to a rough, little cabin on the edge of the desert with an unlatched door. No one answered when she knocked, so she opened the door and looked inside. A bright little fire burned on the hearth, and a chair stood ready by the side of a table on which food was spread. A note lay beside the plate with her name on it! Opening it she read:

"It is God which girdeth me with strength, and maketh my way perfect. Thy right hand hath holden me up, and Thy gentleness hath made me great. Thou hast enlarged my steps under me and my feet did not slip" (Ps. 18:32, 35, 36). And then the words, "Wait on the Lord and be of good courage. Wait here on the Lord, Aletheia, until He shows you what to do."

So outside the walls of Mountain Top City, Aletheia ate the food so graciously provided and lay down and slept peacefully on the little bed. Next morning, when she woke, she was laughing. It seemed to her that she had been in the courts of heaven and had found the angels who greeted her laughing happily. "Aletheia has scrambled over the wall," they told each other merrily. "Rather bruised and sore in body and feelings, but really on the way to the High Places at last. Blessed be He who only doeth wonderous things and blessed be His holy Name."

"No wonder they were laughing, and me with them," said Aletheia to herself happily. "For, really, it is a 'holy joke.' I who have so zealously warned everybody 'outside the city' that they were led astray by 'dangerous errors' and 'unsound doctrine' now have exactly the same things said about myself! Oh, it is as I saw in the vision, that what we do and think and say to others, we really think and say and do to ourselves, too. Let me be warned, from this time forth, to pray for grace to think and say and do to others only what I shall love to have them do and think and say about me!"

5

Outside
the
Camp

Aletheia stayed in the little cabin on the edge of the desert for quite a while, according to the instructions which had been given her. It was not an easy time for her, for the cabin was close to Mountain Top City, and when news got about that Aletheia had, apparently, "leapt over the wall" by night and left the city, some of her friends went to find out what had happened to her and discovered the cabin. Then began a long-drawn-out and sorrowful time of resisting loving entreaties that she should cast aside her dangerous and erroneous new teaching and return to the fold. On the other hand, she was obliged to listen to reproaches and denunciations which deeply wounded her feelings. Moreover, in the zealous determination that none of the other young people who had been helped by Aletheia's enthusiastic witness while she lived in the city be led by her example to leave the blessed safety of Mountain

Top City and go wandering into dangerous bypaths, frequent messages were broadcast through the loudspeakers to the residents of the city warning everyone not to allow themselves to be deceived.

Since Aletheia's little cabin was so close to the city walls, she could not help hearing these broadcast warnings; and her feelings were constantly wounded by them, until sometimes she felt as though her heart was pricked by swords and knives. Again and again she thought of the words of another wounded soul who had written and sung, "I lie even among them that are set on fire, even the sons of men, whose teeth are spears and arrows, and their tongue a sharp sword" (Ps. 57:4).

Sometimes, too, anonymous messages were sent, often causing her real anguish of heart. They accused her, not of being deluded into error, but of actually wanting to set herself up as an inspired prophetess or messenger from God who desired to outshine all His true and faithful messengers who were loyal to the one true and precious Truth entrusted to the custody of the inhabitants and leaders in Mountain Top City.

These accusations not only had the power to wound Aletheia more than anything else, but they troubled her mind and filled it with questions and doubts. Was it possible that she really *was* being deceived, and that the wondrous thing which she thought she had seen she had only imagined? Didn't the Book of Truth actually say that "the heart of man is deceitful above all things and desperately wicked"? Then how likely it was that her stupendous and glorious new illumination of a far higher conception of the Nature of God and of His love than she had been able to see before was, after all, a "false imagination" of her own heart—even though it had inflamed her with a far greater love for Him and trust in His goodness than the former beliefs about Him had been able to do. For how could all those devoted and earnest spiritual leaders in Mountain Top City have remained unaware of this glorious revelation of God's nature and love if it were really true?

For a time these questions caused her real agony of mind. One day she rose very early and went to the trysting place east of the great rock barrier from which—far, far away in the distance—she could glimpse the shining peaks of the High Places. As she stood there gazing longingly at their far-off glories, she stretched her arms towards them and cried out appealingly: "O my Lord, show me how I can know what is true and what is false. How can I distinguish between truth and error, so that I may not be deceived or become a stumbling block to others?"

Then, as though a beautiful and gentle voice actually spoke to her from those faraway heights of glory, there came shining into her mind the words that the Prince of Truth had actually spoken Himself:

"Ye shall know the false prophets from the true by their fruits. . . . A good tree cannot bring forth evil fruit, neither can a corrupt tree bring forth good fruit. Wherefore by their fruits ye shall know them" (Matt. 7:15-20). "Ye shall know the Truth and the Truth shall make you free" (John 8:32).

"Aletheia, you can only distinguish truth from error in one way: namely, by the fruits that follow in your own life and the lives of those who proclaim what they call truth. That is, if the new illumination gives you the power to love and trust God more than you did before; to love all your fellow men in the One Body of Mankind; and to long to treat them only as you wish to be treated yourself; this is how you may discern the truth. If you are able to love even those who wound your feelings and misconstrue your intentions; to accept it all with no resentment, bitterness, or self-pity, but with praise and thanksgiving, just as Jesus would; if this new belief raises you to a still higher level of love than you had reached before, then you may be sure that what you have seen is not false, but a part of a higher truth that you have not yet seen fully. Then you are free from all thought, attitudes, and reactions to others which are unlike those which Jesus taught are not correct for people living in the Kingdom of Heaven.

"It is possible, however, that in the future you may believe that you have been shown a yet higher facet of

truth and find yourself reacting to reproaches and misunderstanding with resentment or anger. You may begin to feel superior to others and to forget that even
those who attack you are members of the One Body of
Mankind in whom the Lord of Love is also conscious.
You may begin to belittle or to denounce them and to
exalt yourself in your own thoughts. Then you may well
doubt whether the new supposed truth is true after all.
For only what is true itself can deliver you and set you
free from everything which is not of the truth, and
which is unlike the Ideal of the Kingdom of Heaven.
So, remember, you can only discern between truth and
falsity, the good and the evil, by the attitudes, reactions,
and way of life which they awaken in you as you accept
them."

At this Aletheia was immensely comforted, and the
burden on her heart rolled away. For she knew that
although she was almost daily wounded by the reproaches she received, and though they hurt her feelings greatly, yet she did still love her friends in Mountain Top City. She would always be grateful for the
blessings which they had so lovingly shared with her,
and the truths into which they had led her at the beginning of her journey to the High Places of Love and
Truth. Mountain Top City had been the first beautiful
stepping stone towards the glorious heights which,
with her whole heart, she yearned to reach. Nothing

could ever cancel the debt of love and gratitude she owed the people there or diminish her love towards them.

From that time onwards, whenever painful questions returned, she checked with her own heart to see if she still had power to remain loving and unresentful and was able to bear and forgive with joy, praise, and thanksgiving. Finding that it was so, she rejoiced that she might keep and prize her lovely new treasure and illumination. Increasingly, it was so precious that all that she had apparently lost seemed worthless in comparison. She realized, too, that all the wounded feelings were really wounded pride, and that nothing—least of all true love—can be hurt by anything. "The only thing in me that can be hurt," she told herself, "is hurt Pride. And the sooner that is pushed out of the way, the better."

However, in spite of the fact that victory was given to her again, the emotional strain and suffering through which she had passed began to tell upon Aletheia's health. Suddenly, she became ill and lay alone in the little cabin, tossing with fever and weak from a hemorrhage. Those who visited the cabin, though they truly sought to help her and to nurse her, could only add to her bewilderment and distress by saying, "There you are! This is what happens to you when you turn aside from the truth and stubbornly refuse to repent and to seek God's forgiveness. This would not have happened to you, you may be sure, if God really wished to confirm that your guidance was right. It is clearly His warning to you that you have been deluding yourself."

It was a case of "Job's friends" all over again. "There you are! Admit now that you are in the wrong, for who has known the godly to be forsaken and afflicted and without God's supporting help and deliverance?"

At first it was almost too much for Aletheia to bear. But just at that lowest point of all, when all things seemed to be against her, a wonderful joy and peace flowed into her soul daily as she sought to bear it all with forgiveness and to overcome self-pity. Her mind was completely at peace as she realized that the King of Love Himself was experiencing it all with her, just as she had seen in her glorious vision of the Abyss of Love. She became certain that He was preparing a glorious deliverance of some kind. She then began to recover her health rapidly and to feel certin that deliverance was near.

One day when she had almost completely recovered her strength again, there was a knock on the door of the cabin. This time a stranger entered, and the first thing she noticed was that on his forehead was inscribed the beautiful name which she had seen engraved in the forehead of the first messenger who had opened for her the door leading to the vision of the Abyss of Love.

The strange visitor greeted her gently, saying that he had learned about her through the messages being broadcast from Mountain Top City, and that he had come to see if he could offer assistance in any way.

The gentleness and kindness in his face and voice so comforted Aletheia that she opened her heart and shared with him the whole story of the glorious vision which had transformed all her ideas and beliefs about God, of the leap or scramble over the wall, and of all that had happened since.

"It is strange," she said finally, "that in the end I should have fallen ill and so given those who disbelieved in the vision grounds to claim that God was punishing me for presumptuous pride and self-will. Why do you think this was allowed to happen to me?"

Her visitor put out his hand and, gently taking hers, said, "Aletheia, I will tell you why. It is not punishment. God never punishes. And He well knows how you have been longing to do His will. This sickness has been given you as a loving message to help you understand that there was a *still higher and more heavenly way* of reacting to the wounds and troubles that you were experiencing than you knew about. Certainly God gave you a glorious victory even though your feelings were so wounded; you were delivered from resentment and were able to accept it all with forgiveness. But perhaps there was a little self-pity because you did not realize about the glorious principle I have been sent to share with you. For there is a still higher level of acceptance possible, and that is to accept everything that happens with praise, thanksgiving, and joy, knowing that every seeming affliction is really a blessing in disguise. God allows only the very best things possible to happen to you at any particular time; that is to say, exactly the things and situations that are best fitted to help you, because they afford you the opportunity of reacting just as Jesus did. Learning by His grace to react with praise and thanksgiving even to things that appear most evil, unjust, cruel, and deplorable, because God is allowing this opportunity to bring good out of evil, is just like waving a magic wand over an evil enchantment and being able to replace cruel spells with heavenly miracles.

"That is why you were allowed to become ill, Aleth-eia, beloved child of God. Through the temple of the Holy Spirit, your own body, you have been allowed to learn about this glorious principle and not only to receive complete healing, but to understand how to avoid sickness and disease symptoms in the future."

Then he added with a little laugh, "So now you will know that whenever any physical symptom of dis-ease, pain, or sickness begins to appear in your own body, it is a gentle touch from the Great Physician and Healer. He is calling you into His consulting room so that He may have the opportunity of showing you how to react to whatever trials or testings may be besetting you, in a higher, more perfect, and Christ-like way than you have been able to do."

Aletheia stared at him with tears of joy in her eyes, and he added still more gently, "Learn, too, from this experience to be very, very gentle with other sincere, devoted, and good people who are sick or suffering in any way in their bodies. Never suggest that they are in any way to blame, nor try to convict them of some error in conduct. Simply realize that, like yourself, they have been passing through a time of sore trial and attacks on the great battlefield of life and have received grievous wounds. Like you, too, they did not know about this glorious principle of reacting to everything with praise and thanksgiving, seeking a still more triumphant and heavenly way of reacting. Remember, they have probably been, and are, bearing burdens such as you yourself could hardly bear to contemplate. Never judge or blame anyone, only feel the utmost love, compassion, and desire to share the higher healing principle with them, too.

"And now, Aletheia, I have to tell you that I have been sent to show you the way to start on your journey to those glorious, shining High Places which have been beckoning and calling to you for so long. Come with me and I will show you the path to follow."

*"Let us go forth therefore unto Him without
the Camp, bearing His reproach!"*
Heb. 13:13

"Outside the Camp" with Christ, let's go
Leap over manmade walls,
Onto the rubbish heap we'll throw
Our fetters when He calls.
    And new and higher truths we'll find
    That free us from the things that bind.

Concepts of God we find can't be
The best to help us now.
Methods and ways we've come to see
To manmade doctrines bow.
    Let's lift our eyes, new heights behold
    And greater glories than the old.

Our friends and neighbors may accuse
And say we've error found;
To listen to us they'll refuse
Misunderstanding will abound.
    The wounds will heal, we'll work and live
    If we a faithful witness give.

At first there may be loneliness
Out in the desert bare,
But very soon we shall confess
Our Lord is with us there.
    Far greater joys and power we'll find,
    Freedom from doubt and peace of mind.

Be humble, willing to abide
In "Secret Service," so
Safe in the freedom here outside
A higher life we'll know.
    "Unseen by men" we'll safely stand,
    Hidden in God—held in His hand.

The loneliness will pass indeed,
New friendships we shall share,
And God will give us all we need
With tender, loving care.
    Lay down the old and clasp the new,
    Its fruits bear witness it is true.

It's by its fruits that Truth is known,
And by its blessings too.
We practice what the Lord has shown
And find that it is true.
    It helps us to forgive and love
    And God gives graces from above.

Yes, go outside the Camp, be free!
Leap over manmade walls,
Forsake the less, the better see,
And follow where Christ calls.
    To Higher Places He has trod,
    To closer union with our God.

6

The Way of Holiness

With what joy Aletheia went forth with the new messenger who had been sent to her so graciously! He led her eastwards over the desert until they came to a "strait and narrow" highway running directly towards the radiant High Places which had beckoned to her in such a compelling fashion that she had left all to go forth and journey to them. On this highway her friend left her, saying with a beautiful smile, that he too was called to still Higher Places, but by a short cut; and that one day they would meet again and behold the still Higher and renew their fellowship together.

As she pursued her way along the highway, Aletheia found to her joy that she had a number of companions on the road, all pressing towards the shining heights that lay ahead. Although from Mountain Top City that glorious range of beckoning mountains had looked so lofty and distant that it seemed as though it must belong to another and higher world altogether, Aletheia was overjoyed to find that it was not nearly so long and difficult a journey as she had expected. It was made all the shorter by the delightful and happy companionship with others, especially after the loneliness of her experiences outside the Camp.

One day the highway led them straight up to the green foothills over which the white peaks towered heavenwards in all their glory, and on those green pasturelands there was a School for Studying Heavenly Knowledge. The residents from the shining heights above came down daily and held classes at which all those who had made the journey there were welcome to attend. So for a time Aletheia and her friends lived together in little white cottages on the hillside and went to the School of Heavenly Knowledge for daily instruction. Here they were taught about the Kingdom of Heaven Way of Life which would be theirs when they were able to live on those blessed and happy regions above the green alps.

Here is a brief outline of the chief principles of the Heavenly Life which Aletheia and her friends were taught. "The road which led you here," said these teachers, "is called 'The Way of Holiness' (Isa. 35:8), and in these daily classes we are to have the privilege of teaching you how to live as HOLY PEOPLE by devoting yourselves to expressing only what is GOOD, unmixed with

anything which is NOT GOOD, namely evil. We will teach
you how to refuse every temptation to listen to, or
think, or to speak, or read about, the things which are
not good. Here you are to learn the glorious secret of A
TRANSFORMED-THOUGHT LIFE, summed up in these words,
'Fill your minds with those things which are good and
deserve praise, things that are true, right, pure, lovely
and honorable' (Phil. 4:8, NEB). You will also learn to
react in thought to everything that happens to you and
to every person you meet in the way that the inhabitants
of the Kingdom of Heaven do, and which Jesus taught
and demonstrated so perfectly.

"For you must realize and understand that *your
thought life is your real life* and creates the only real world
in which you live. 'As a man thinketh in his heart, so he
is,' and so he appears to God and the Holy Angels in the
spiritual world. The things that you say, do, and picture
to yourself and to others in the inner world of your
thoughts, are the real things that God hears and sees
you saying and doing. What you later do through your
physical bodies is only the fruit of what you have first
said and done in your true, spiritual body. Oh, how
important it is that you should understand this and
constantly remind yourself that God sees you as a spiritual being, using for a time a little, physical body as an
instrument through which to express the thoughts and
desires of your heart or spiritual being. Perhaps it may

help you to think of yourselves as spiritual beings, carrying about with you, as a man may do, a little 'walkie-talkie' instrument (your body) by means of which to communicate with other spirits also learning to use earthly bodies or instruments on this planet. In the spiritual world, though, you are all freely in communication by means of your spiritual bodies, and there you act and react to each other in *thought*.

"Then you must also understand that *your thoughts create your feelings and your desires.* As you think in the inner world of your heart, so you will feel and desire; and those feelings and desires will determine what you will say and do through the 'walkie-talkie' of your physical body.

"Then you must realize something very important indeed. What the 'INNER MAN' (Eph. 3:16) or spirit expresses through the instrument or 'walkie-talkie' of the body—namely, the desires and feelings expressed in behavior to others and your reactions to all that happens to you—all these things continually modify and rebuild your physical bodies, making all the living cells in those bodies, and constantly replacing those which are dying and being expelled from the body with new ones, stamped with the likeness of all the thoughts and desires you are expressing. Indeed, from head to foot your physical bodies are the visible or earthly form in which all your spiritual thoughts, desires, and emotions are manifest—literally, *forms* of thought and desire expressing the nature of the 'inner man,' or thinker."

At this point in the lesson, Aletheia and her companions literally gasped with astonishment, but their teacher went on quietly:

"As I have just told you, you will quickly find that your thoughts determine your feelings, and accordingly, your *feelings*, in a very special way, react in and through your physical body or instrument. Therefore, it is very important indeed that you create only holy and loving feelings in your inner thought world. This you can best do by learning to give a beautiful and good name to everything that happens to you through your physical body on earth, as well as to what other spirits do to you through their bodies and cause you to experience in yours.

"For example, if you tell yourself in thought that something is happening or going to happen which is fearful and dreadful, you will *feel* fear and dread. If you tell yourself in thought that people are acting in an annoying and irritating way, annoyed and irritated you will *feel*. If you call anyone selfish in your thoughts, selfish you will find them. For whatever *name* you give to anything in thought, that it will become for you. Therefore, learn to give everything a beautiful and good name, and you will feel only happy and blessed. Giving a beautiful and good name to everything means that you will feel and experience only good, beautiful, and blessed things. It may be difficult for you to believe this, but if you develop this glorious, heavenly habit of giving good and right names to everything, you will find that this is true.

"Again, for example, if you see or meet with something which seems a dark negation or opposite of true good, learn to call it 'a beautiful opportunity' to react to it in the good way. Express yourself in the form of goodness which it seems to caricature, and by so doing, you will cause the real good to become manifest instead of its dark shadow or negative form. If you meet with selfishness, joyfully call it a chance to be unselfish yourself. Practice the unselfish attitude which is so obviously lacking in some particular person or situation, and lovely, unselfish things will begin springing up all around you. Instead of saying in thought, 'what irritating, thoughtless neighbors,' begin calling them to yourself 'delightful, potential friends and companions.' Just as though you wave a magic wand over them, they will certainly become that if you persist long enough, or else they will move away and be replaced by delightful companions. For you are waving a magic wand over yourself, remember, changing yourself into the nature of the name you give, so that people of the same nature will gravitate to you.

"That, of course, is the whole secret and key. What

you think, you yourself become in spirit. Spirits are continually attracted to, and gravitating towards, other spirits that think, desire, and feel the same kind of things as themselves. To think only of good things continually attracts other good and loving spirits to you in the real world of spirit or thought as you strengthen and bless one another. The reverse happens if you think and feel unkind or unloving things. As spirits carry their bodies or 'walkie-talkies' with them, so you will find yourselves continually drawn to those whose thoughts are all devoted to goodness only. Just, in fact, as you have all been drawn to one another here for these classes.

"Remember, too, that as men and women think in their hearts, so they will express those thoughts in some way. THOUGHT CANNOT BE HIDDEN. It will 'out' and manifest its nature. You cannot whisper anything to yourself in your inner thought world, either good or evil, but sooner or later 'it will be shouted from the rooftop'; that is, be expressed in some way either in, or through, your body.

"All this shows you why THE WAY OF HOLINESS—consecrating yourself to goodness only—is so vitally important, and why the Lord God so impressed it upon the consciousness and conscience of Adam and Eve, the representatives of Mankind in the Garden of Eden. In that beautiful, first Ideal life, there was only one 'thou shalt not,' and that was 'Thou shalt not eat of the Tree of the Knowledge of Good and Evil'; that is, have nothing to do with anything which has evil mixed with the good. What you know would not be good or happy for you to experience, do not cause anyone else to experience it. Love and treat everyone in the good way in which you long to be loved and treated yourself; and do nothing to others that you would not like done, said, or thought about you. Never mix a grain of evil with the good, but consecrate yourselves to expressing good only. The Fall of Mankind was breaking this great commandment and acting to other living creatures in the Garden in ways one would not like to be treated oneself—introducing evil things along with the good and happy things.

"What is goodness? It is the very nature of God Himself, Who is THE ETERNAL WILL TO TREAT EVERY CREATURE HE BRINGS INTO EXISTENCE AS HE WOULD LIKE TO BE TREATED HIMSELF; IT IS WISE LOVE. It is a passion to make all living souls happy and to cause them to experience the best possible joy and blessedness in a way that will develop the capacity to receive more and still higher forms of joy and goodness.

"This is why we so joyfully come down to teach you these blessed things, so that you too may soon be able to rise to a still higher level of wise love and goodness and greater power in expressing and increasing it. This will help you understand what will happen in the 'temple' of your physical body if, through ignorance or self-will, this wonderful Law of Holiness is broken, and you begin to mix evil with good. For then you will sow the seeds of dis-ease and sickness in your bodies, just as the Lord warned Adam in the Garden of Eden. It is evil mixed with good which turns immortal bodies into corruptible, mortal ones, subject to destruction and death.

"If human beings were not clothed in 'coats of skins' (Gen. 3:21), as they have been ever since their Fall into evil, they would still have beautiful, transparent bodies as was the case before the Fall. You would be able to see at once in your own bodies and into those of others the consequences of beginning to think about and desire something not good, and then of expressing it in some way in word and action and behavior. You would perceive at once how the perfect harmony in the functioning of the different organs of the body is destroyed as the cells and organisms begin to reflect those unkind attitudes and cause the first symptoms of 'dis-ease' and failure to cooperate lovingly together in the perfect way they should.

"For example, it is possible to see almost at once the unhappy and harmful results which follow speaking in anger or condemnation or contempt to, or about, someone else, or the results which begin to manifest almost at once in some area of the body as soon as unkind or selfish actions have been done. The nature of those words and actions begins to impress its likeness on some of the cells of the body. They begin to change from holy, harmless, innocent cells into unhealthy and harmful ones, acting like minute, wild beasts and attacking and hurting the other cells around them.

"In very truth every cell and organism in your body bears the 'image or superscription' or likeness of the nature of the one who speaks and acts; the image either of 'God-inspired' words and actions or of self-inspired ones. Habitual thoughts, attitudes, and reactions continue to impress their likeness on more and more cells, either for good or ill. Finally, the body becomes increasingly filled with light cells, manifesting holy health and harmony, or with dark cells that cause symptoms of chronic disease and crippling disorders.

"When this happens, how blessed it is to know that if the Holy Spirit is allowed to change the unkind attitudes, feelings, and desires into holy, loving, forgiving ones, the likeness of these good expressions of thought and desire will at once begin to stamp their likeness on the new cells. These are continually replacing the old ones and in time will bring healing and maintain holy health. However, true holiness must be practiced by consecrating oneself to expressing good only with no evil of any kind mixed with it. If you keep yourselves open continually to receive new light and to respond whenever a still higher level of possible goodness is revealed to you, all the cells will become light cells.

"You must also remember that, as the years pass, you will reach periods in your life when your spiritual development should be capable of perceiving and responding to higher levels of truth and goodness than it was able to perceive during the earlier periods, just as all of you who have reached these green alps at the foot of the High Places are able to see what your friends and companions are not yet capable of perceiving. But whenever a higher understanding of the Truth begins to shine into your hearts, always open to it to the fullest possible extent, and respond to it, no matter how costly it may seem to do so. For only so will you be able to continue developing in holiness and be ready to be led up to a still higher level of God-consciousness and power.

"But if you count the cost too great and reject the new light, you will inevitably find that you begin to lose your spiritual power and sensitivity to light, and that the Way of Holiness becomes impossible for you. Your thought, attitudes, words, and actions will gradually become more and more negative, and your bodies correspondingly filled with unhealthy, weak, and chronically diseased cells. Especially will this be the case as old age approaches. For that is the period of life when you should be ripening in a specially beautiful way in readiness for the new heavenly bodies which you hope to receive. But this is not possible if, somewhere along the journey thither, a higher light shone upon you, and you rejected or did not respond to it in full obedience.

"Therefore, beloved pupils and seekers for the High Places of Truth, be ever on the watch. As soon as even the smallest symptoms of dis-ease or disharmony begin to manifest in your bodies or minds, go into the full light of God's Presence and let His Holy Spirit gently, faithfully, and lovingly point out to you where a still holier thought, attitude, or reaction is necessary if perfect Holy Health is to be maintained in the temple of the Holy Spirit—your body. Then you will find healing and be able to demonstrate the 'beauty of Holiness and of Holy Health in your own lives, encouraging and challenging others to follow the same blessed Way.' "

7

The Dangerous Pinnacles

These classes given by the people from the Higher Places did not last all day long. All the eager pupils were urged by their teachers to go out each afternoon to practice and test out the wonderful teachings they had received in the mornings. At this point, perhaps, it will be well to give a word of explanation. Time on the High Places is not the same as ordinary earth time, and if in this book, for example, it is suggested that Aletheia and her companions spent several weeks in the classrooms learning the higher Heavenly Knowledge, it really means that in terms of earthly time calculations, several years passed by. On the slopes or lower alps of the High Places, where these classes were held, one day might equal a week or month of earth time. They were told that when the time came for them to go "farther on and higher up" to yet Higher Places, they would find that one day there was like a year of earth time; the higher they were able to go, the greater the difference in time periods would become, until, on the really Highest Places one day would be like a thousand years of earth time. So many wonderful things could be accomplished in one day up there on those levels that a thousand years would not suffice to accomplish them down on the earthly levels far below.

Moreover, their teachers told them that even on the slightly Higher Places than those which they had reached at that time, processes which would need weeks or months of earth time to accomplish or bring to fruition could be completed in a few moments or even instantaneously; and such processes were called by ordinary people on earth, "miraculous happenings" or "signs and wonders."

Of course, all the earnest seekers for Truth in the classrooms with Aletheia were as eager as herself to go on to reach the still higher levels of miraculous power, but they were gently told by their teachers that before they could be permitted to do so and to be entrusted with the use of these Higher Powers, they must learn to use and share with others the present knowledge which was being imparted to them. Then they would know whether they were really fit to receive the still higher knowledge and the privilege of being permitted to make contact with and use the higher powers of the Kingdom of Heaven levels.

So every afternoon they went forth joyfully in groups or two by two, sharing the lessons which they had been learning with those in the green pastures and the lower foothills who were willing to listen to them.

To her wondering joy Aletheia discovered that there were many people who had reached those blessed pasturelands but were not yet able to attend the School for Heavenly Knowledge. They were thankful and delighted to hear as much as the happy students were able to share with them, and she had more opportunities to teach and witness to attentive and responsive hearers. Aletheia remembered their experiences in Mountain Top City, where so often they had been forced to offer their earnest messages to empty streets and closed doors, or only to their own fellow inhabitants in the city. She realized with awed thanksgiving that, as a result of her costly leap over the wall, she now had increasing opportunities to witness freely to responsive hearers about the glorious truth which had so transformed her own life and development. For all the time more and more people came to listen, and invitations from places farther and farther away were reaching her; and her heart overflowed with thankful joy. It seemed to her that all that she had been asked to lay down into death, and all the happy fellowship she had left behind, was now being raised up and restored to her a hundredfold, and in a far more glorious form than before.

Her beloved teachers told her that this blessed and glorious Heavenly Principle must be shared with others: EVERYTHING VOLUNTARILY LAID DOWN INTO DEATH IN OBEDIENT RESPONSE TO THE VISION OF A YET HIGHER TRUTH, WILL BE RAISED UP IN SOME YET MORE GLORIOUS FORM. Everything left in obedience to a call from God will be restored a hundredfold.

One day it seemed to her that this glorious principle was fulfilled in full perfection. She heard her name called by a well-known voice, felt her hands clasped, and found herself looking into the face of Zeal—her beloved friend, companion and helper from Mountain Top City.

"Aletheia!" he exclaimed, "I simply had to follow! When you left and I remembered your faithful courageous witness to the higher Truth that you had seen, I could find no rest. At last—and, oh, I regret I did not do it sooner—I, too, went outside the gate to the great rock barricade at the east of the city. There the Door of Vision was opened to me, also, and like you, I saw what I can never unsee. So then 'I was not disobedient to the heavenly vision,' but leaped over the wall too, and went outside the camp 'bearing His reproach.' Now, here I am, by the grace of God, permitted to learn, work, and witness with you once again. For surely, Aletheia, Love of Truth and Zeal in witness to the Truth should work together hand in hand. It is God who has brought us together again."

Oh what unspeakable joy and gratitude filled the heart of Aletheia as she looked into his face. But as each day passed she could not help recognizing that it was a changed Zeal supporting her in their happy work. His face was so much more gentle, so full of loving tenderness as he witnessed to those who gathered to listen, and all the stern, young dogmatism had vanished—fallen, too, perhaps, into the ground to die, just like everything else that he had left behind in Mountain Top City in order to find the Higher Places.

A number of weeks and months of time in the schoolroom passed in radiant happiness, in blessed hours of learning, and blessed hours of witnessing and sharing with all who gathered to listen. These came in greater and greater numbers, and Aletheia and Zeal received so many invitations to go to other places to share the lessons that they hardly knew how to respond to them all.

Gradually, and at first almost imperceptibly, Aletheia found that a subtle change was taking place in herself. The joy of so many opportunities to share the truths which others had rejected was becoming almost an intoxicating pleasure. She found herself instinctively watching to see how many gathered to listen, exulting in the rapidly increasing numbers. Then, almost as imperceptively, she found herself on the alert to see if the groups of listeners who gathered around her companions on the neighboring slopes were bigger than those who came to listen to her, and whether she was gradually attracting more listeners than they were. Zeal too shared in this mild, but increasingly heady and intoxicating pleasure. They accepted more and more invitations, until Aletheia began to feel completely exhausted. At such times Zeal encouraged her to "rest in the Lord" and to remember that His strength would be made perfect in her weakness. But Aletheia found herself less and less able to rest or sleep, and more and more mentally and nervously depleted; yet more and more people were waiting to be attended to and helped.

In order to lessen the strain of so many teaching and preaching engagements, they began studying which ones seemed to be the most important because they would afford the opportunity to share the Heavenly Teaching with the greatest number of people. This meant that they soon refused all invitations to visit only small groups; the time for personal work and counseling with needy people was cut almost to the minimum.

All this busy witness and traveling to other places was possible because of a vacation from the classes in the School of Heavenly Knowledge. Aletheia's teacher had told her and Zeal, with a loving but rather strange expression on his face, that now they would learn more by having a vacation from the classes, and that they were not to return until further notice.

Aletheia began to feel more and more troubled in

spirit, as well as physically and mentally exhausted, but she did not seem able to alter the situation.

One day Zeal came to her with a look of intense and excited exultation on his face. He took her hand, saying, "Come with me," and led her away from the green slopes to a more distant hilltop. It was crowned with a great rock pinnacle in the shape of a high and imposing-looking seat overlooking an arenalike hillside, where a thousand or more people could easily gather and listen. "See," said Zeal exultantly, "we have received an invitation to share our blessed, heavenly teaching even from this pinnacle dais—a privilege and expression of appreciation and trust offered only to greatly loved and revered teachers and leaders."

As he spoke his eyes glittered in a strange way, and he looked like a man under the influence of a strong, intoxicating excitement. Aletheia, too, for a moment felt an intoxicating pleasure coursing through her veins. Then her heart sank in the strangest way, and she could not utter a word in response. She allowed Zeal to lead her up to the pinnacle seat and dais. From there she caught sight of other hilltops in the neighborhood, each with its own pinnacle rock seat, and instinctively she looked to see if any were higher and afforded greater elevation than the one to which he was leading her.

They reached the rocky dais. There was no one on the slopes below at that time, and bowing as though in loving homage, Zeal said, "My beloved, let us sit down on this pinnacle of blessed opportunity to which God has led us and offer ourselves to Him anew for this glorious, higher service which He is entrusting to us."

Aletheia sat down silently on the rocky thronelike chair, and as she did so a dread chill and darkness settled upon her. It was as though something deep within her soul was striving to express some message, to give a warning. But what was it?

Then, almost like an echo of Zeal's words, "*Higher* Service," came the thought of the Higher Places. She raised her eyes and looked upwards as had become habitual to her when seeking help, looking for the High Places. And then, with a shock, she realized the truth. The pinnacle seat on which she was sitting faced westwards, not eastwards. Sitting there, no matter how she might lift her eyes and look upwards, she would not be able to see the High Places, for her back was towards them. She could see nothing higher than the pinnacle rock itself.

With a little, gasping sob she at last broke the silence. "Zeal," she cried tremblingly, "I cannot accept the invitation we have received. It means turning our backs on the Higher Places, looking only at what is happening and being offered to us, not at the Truth. Let me tell you something that happened to me only yesterday, Zeal. A poor woman in deep distress came to me seeking spiritual counsel, because I was entrusted, so she had heard, with a message of very good news for all in distress. But I felt so tired and strained, and under such pressure, that I simply could not spare the time to help her. So I gently put my hand on her shoulder and said, 'Today I simply have no time to spare for you. Perhaps tomorrow it will be possible. God Himself will help and bless you if you ask Him to do so.'

"She just looked me in the face and said quietly, 'It is today that I need God's help. I was told that you were one of His messengers who would help me to make contact with His power. But you—you looked at me as if you didn't even see me.' "

Saying this Aletheia burst into passionate tears. "She said, 'You looked at me as though you didn't even see me,' " she repeated, and then cried in anguish, "It was true, I didn't really see her, only myself and my own important and pressing affairs, and she was no one important, just one amongst a multitude of other people for whom I had no time to spare. Oh! what has happened to me?" She stood up, trembling from head to foot. "Lord, rescue me!" she cried, and then, before Zeal could stop her, she began running down the hillside. After a moment she tripped and fell headlong, but scrambled to her feet, bruised and dazed, and continued running haltingly and stumblingly down the hill.

"Where are the High Places?" cried Aletheia. "Lord,

help me. Send forth Thy Truth and Thy Light and let them lead me and bring me to Thy Holy Hill."

Then stumbling into the house where she was staying, she went to her room, locked the door, and fell on the bed, sobbing as though her heart would break.

8
The
Groaning
Creation

Very, very early next morning, while it was yet dark, Aletheia left her room and looked up at the dark mountain slopes towards the peaks silhouetted dimly against the faint eastern light. Then she began running up the mountainside, just as her mother, Grace-and-Glory, had done along the slopes of the High Places on her "hinds' feet." Now her daughter found that she too had developed the legs and hooves of the mountain gazelles, and could leap and bound from rock to rock and over the snowy slopes as lightly and swiftly as they could.

Just as she leapt towards the last rocky crag, a crimson glow outlined it as the shining orb of the sun appeared. At the next moment she was standing on the topmost peak, a tiny speck against the dawn-lit sky.

Then she caught her breath. For there, from the summit of those High Places which from Mountain Top

City had looked so far distant and unattainable, she saw towering into the heavens, as though belonging to another world altogether, a range of mountain peaks more dazzlingly white and glorious than anything she had conceived of before. Ranges of yet Higher Places of Truth and Goodness in the Nature of God Who is the Eternal Will to Goodness only.

Aletheia stood there and looked, panting from her eager longing to rush up the mountainside, and her heart was sick almost unto death with the longing that filled it for that yet higher world shining in the dawn-light far, far above.

Then once again, just as when a little child, she lifted her arms and cried yearningly, "Lord, turn them into wings—eagles' wings on which to fly to the Higher Places."

But instead, a cold, thick mist descended on the peak and mountain range on which she was standing, enveloping her in a veil or cold shroud so that soon she could see nothing at all, not even the steep, slippery track up which she had bounded to the summit. She found herself alone in the mist and cold of a bitter, sunless mountain peak. Everything was blotted out around her, and there was not a sound of any kind—human, bird, or beast. She was alone and in the dark.

Suddenly, she understood. "This is what will happen to me if I accept the invitation to sit on that rock pinnacle seat high above others but with my back to the High

Places. O my Lord, rescue me. Lead me not into temptation but deliver me from evil."

There was a crashing peal of thunder, a blinding flash of lightning which ripped the veil of mist asunder from top to bottom, and Aletheia found that once again she was standing on the edge of the Abyss of Love. Before her lay the mighty cross, stretched out from end to end of the great canyon.

Only now as she gazed at it she saw something which she had not seen when she had looked upon it for the first time and found her whole life transformed by the vision. This time she saw that the foot of that stupendous cross rested in a manger in a little stable. In the stable were a few sheep with their lambs beside them. An ox was chewing straw at one end of the rude shelter, a donkey was tethered beside the door, and among the rafters roosted a little flock of pigeons. In the manger itself was a little human baby, a tiny "Son of Man" lying amongst the birds and beasts which sheltered in the stable. Just as she perceived this, a rooster on the roof of the stable uttered a loud and long-drawn-out crow, calling through the darkness of the night the glad news that daybreak was not far distant. At the sound of the cock-crow the little baby in the manger stirred, wakened, and uttered a feeble little cry. At that the pigeons began a soft and gentle crooning which lulled him off to sleep again.

Bending over the manger cradle in that rude stable,

Aletheia saw a great and glorious angel who beckoned to her and said, "You who love the Truth, come and kneel here and see and understand."

So Aletheia knelt in wondering awe on the rough, stony floor and looked at the little "Son of Man," wrapped deep in the straw of the bed made for him. The angel said, "Here lies the little 'Son of Man,' born to represent the whole Race of Fallen Mankind on the great cross of their self-created sufferings. But he is also 'the Son of God' because he represents the first glorious and Ideal Mankind made in God's image and likeness as was the first Man Adam who is the Son of God (Luke 3:38). This lost Ideal, from which Mankind fell so long ago, will be revealed once again to all who have eyes to see and hearts willing to respond and return to that perfect and glorious Ideal Way of Life.

"But here, too, in this little stable you see the birds and beasts who were created by the same Heavenly Father Creator as was Man himself. The ox and ass and the gentle, harmless, and innocent living creatures still live according to the Ideal, Garden-of-Eden way of life. They hurt no other creatures and eat only the food ordained by God to be the nourishment of all living creatures—from the vegetable and plant Kingdom. The meek and defenseless sheep, lambs, doves, and pigeons use no force in order to defend themselves.

"See, the little 'Son of Man' is born amongst them in

order to show that He represents all the birds, beasts, and other living creatures—not just the fallen sons of men. His manger cradle is on the cross created by Mankind's sins to show that whatsoever men do to each other they do to Him too; and whatever they do to the other living creatures—the birds, beasts, insects, and creeping things—*they also do to Him.* For He is the Divine Love and Life of God immanent in every living creature in the One Great Body of Creation. Now look, Aletheia, lover of the Truth. Look and behold the Truth."

So saying the angel pointed away from the foot of the cross where the stable and manger were; and Aletheia, as her eyes followed his pointing finger, uttered a cry of horror and anguish and began to tremble from head to foot. For now she saw that the Body stretched upon and nailed to the cross of suffering and woe was not just the Body of fallen human beings, but was also composed of birds, beasts, and other living creatures. All of them, too, were living cells in one Body of diverse forms and functions. She saw that the sufferings experienced by the human cells in that great, groaning Body of Creation were rooted in those which they were continually inflicting upon each other and other living creatures. They exercised a terrible kind of dominion and misused their power most cruelly. They actually devoured myriads of the living cells around them in the way that cancerous growths do in the physical bodies of their victims. She saw that Mankind's abuse of power over the other living cells or creatures was causing the whole groaning Creation to suffer from a frightful disease. It was literally eating away the life of the Body and causing continual death, from which the Body would certainly perish unless healing and deliverance took place.

Continuous, desolate cries of fear, groans, and screams of pain from the tortured Body on the cross came from myriads of living creatures being whipped and beaten, driven and herded to slaughter houses, and dragged over floors swimming with the blood of the victims preceding them. She heard the most pitiful sounds from the hapless poultry in tiny cages in countless "battery houses" all over the civilized Christian world. She saw living poultry suspended by their feet, heads downwards, carried on endless conveyor belts to rows of seats where boys and girls, fresh from school and splashed from head to foot with spurting blood, cut the throats of the living souls dangling before them. Loud, cheerful music blared forth unceasingly to cover over the woeful sounds, distract from the brutal sight, and deaden the thoughts and feelings of the young slaughterers.

She saw human beings, once shining glorious in "the image and likeness of God" doing this instead of exercising a dominion of love over all that He had created; and helping their little brothers and sisters, the beasts and birds, to perform their own special functions in the glorious Body of Creation. She saw fishing ships patrolling the seas, turning the waves red with the blood of harpooned creatures, and huge nets gathering in loads of hapless, living creatures destined to be killed and devoured by the human cells in the Body by means of their superior skill and strength. She saw innocent, helpless baby seals clubbed to death before the eyes of the mother seals, so that human women and mothers by the thousands may walk about in sealskin coats.

She saw the vivisection laboratories in countless medical institutions where unspeakable experiments were continually being carried out on hapless living souls so that human beings might obtain relief from their own sufferings at the expense of the tortured bodies of their fellow living creatures in the Body of Creation.

She saw uncounted millions of tables around the world where human beings sat down to eat different parts of the bodies of captive and slaughtered victims at least twice daily. They, the living cells, nourished themselves upon the corpses of the slaughtered cells, like a monstrous creature literally killing and eating bits of its own body.

She saw—and almost fell to the ground with the

anguish and horror which the sight caused her—myriads of human beings actually celebrating the birth of the Babe in the stable manger at the foot of the cross, by sitting down with loud rejoicings to devour the forcibly fattened bodies of the lambs, poultry, and turkeys that He had come to rescue. Not realizing that what they did to those hapless creatures they were doing to Him, too, they formed His cross of anguish. They celebrated in the cruelest way possible the birth of the Lamb of God who bears and experiences the sins of the whole world and feels the wrongs which all the members of the One Body do to each other.

Then she saw the battlefields and war-torn areas of the world where human beings, after devouring the corpses of their victims like wild beasts, then attack and slaughter their own human brothers and sisters and innocent little children with diabolical armaments invented in hell, like frightful human wild beasts.

Yes, she saw the whole groaning Creation—fish, birds, creeping and swarming creatures, beasts, domesticated animals, and human beings—all torturing one another in terrible ways. They suffered indescribable agonies in wounds, accidents, frightful physical diseases, and woes and miseries of all kinds. She saw that all these sufferings are truly rooted in the willful breaking of the One Great Law of Love, which commands us to love and treat all living souls as ourselves, for what we do to them we truly do to ourselves in our bodies.

Aletheia felt as though she herself were dying and being "born again" as a new creature, rescued from the cross and raised up in the resurrection Body. She felt herself rising heavenwards at the head of the cross where the face of the One who felt and experienced it all looked at her once again, and the voice of the infinite, suffering, Divine Love of God spoke, saying, "Whatever you do to one of the *least* of these my brethren in the One Body of Creation, YOU ARE DOING TO ME" (Matt. 25:40, 45).

She knew that never again could she inflict suffering on any living creature, nor kill any creature, not even the "least" and smallest insect, nor ever again share in eating the corpses of Mankind's victims. Never again could she use or wear or eat anything taken by force from the bodies of other "living souls," for what she did to the least or greatest of them, she would be doing to the Lord of the Body Himself.

There was the face of the King of Love Himself—the Good Shepherd she had known as a little child, and now "The Lamb of God"—bearing the sufferings and forgiving the sins of the whole world against Himself. Once again His voice challenged her in tones of infinite love and longing: "Aletheia, behold the Truth! Believe it and obey it and live according to the glorious Law of Love. Love Me with all your heart, mind, soul, and strength. Love and treat every creature in the One Great Body of Creation as you want to be loved and treated yourself, for whatever you do to them you do to yourself and Me, also. Never again do to any creature what you would not want done to yourself. What you have now seen you must share with your human brothers and sisters so that they too may 'Know the Truth and the Truth will set them free,' both from inflicting suffering on the groaning Body of Creation and from experiencing suffering as a consequence themselves. 'For the whole creation groaneth, waiting for the manifestation of the Sons of God' (Rom. 8:22, 19). They are waiting for the restoration of Fallen Mankind to the Perfect Ideal from which they have fallen, so that once again they will exercise a Dominion of Perfect Love over the whole Creation."

Then a swirling veil of mist was drawn over the whole scene, which vanished like a dream, in the bright morning sunlight which then spread around her. Aletheia went down the mountainside, knowing that she was not the same person who had ascended the slopes in the early dawn light. She had been baptized into a new understanding and now would live on a new and higher level of life, completely separated from all the cruel customs of the world.

As she reached the green slopes at the foot of those High Places of vision, she caught sight of the rocky

pinnacle seat on which she had so recently been tempted to sit, with her back to the Higher Places and the
new transforming Truth. She shuddered and then wept
with joy and thankfulness at her deliverance.

Then the challenge rang through her soul. "I have
seen the Truth, and now I must witness to it."

9
The Journey Eastward

So began a new and yet still more wonderful phase in Aletheia's journey towards the still Higher Places. Like all new beginnings, it was, at first, both difficult and costly—this time even more so than leaving Mountain Top City. As soon as she began to witness to what she had seen from the summit of those High Places above the green slopes and pasturelands, there was intense consternation and dismay amongst the many groups who had been so eager to listen to her. What was this completely new teaching which no one else in those parts had ever heard of, and which no one else taught? Of course, in other places, Aletheia knew, there must be multitudes of lovers of the Truth who had already ascended the heights and seen the same challenging and awesome truth long before she did.

The difficulty now was not just that the teaching was so new; it called, in fact, for a complete revolution in the accustomed way of life of all who were willing to respond to it. It meant laying aside customs and accepted beliefs which seemed to have had religious sanctions for them from time immemorial. It was a call to cease using, completely and irrevocably, everything taken by force from other living creatures; and to abstain from the use of anything which had caused death or suffering even to the least of all creatures, because everything done to them was done also to the Head of the Body, to the Divine Creator Himself. "Thou shalt not kill" any living creature for any purpose whatsoever completely repudiated all the long-accepted customs, lifetime habits, and religious beliefs of all those diverse groups who had so eagerly listened to Aletheia's earlier messages. It seemed impossible for anyone to respond to such a challenge.

Were they to eat no flesh of any kind at all, not even fish? Could they eat no eggs either because of the unspeakable cruelty of modern "factory farming" practices? Could they not wear clothes made from wool if they did not know whether it had been shorn from hapless victims on the way to the slaughterhouses? Could they wear no leather shoes nor bags made from the skins of dead corpses? Could they not wear fur coats nor use pillows and cushions stuffed with feathers from the dead or not-yet-dead bodies of the poultry and birds? Not only the eating habits of a lifetime must

be changed; one's whole wardrobe, household furnish-
ings, and everything else had to be scrutinized, and, if
necessary, laid aside altogether.

No one would accept this message. No one would
say anything, therefore, to pierce the conscience of anyone with the dreadful idea that the loving Lord and
Saviour whom they worshipped so sincerely is actually
immanent, by His Spirit, in all the living creatures we
wrong. What is done to them is done to Him, too, and
nails Him with them to their cross of suffering. No one
would say, "Come out and be separate" from all these
long-accepted and sanctioned religious customs which
involve and permit the killing of other living souls and
the eating of their dead corpses, in order to follow "the
holy harmless" Lamb of God (Heb. 7:26), who represents all fallen Mankind's innocent and appallingly
wronged victims. No one would say anything about
returning to the glorious, original Ideal from which
Mankind had fallen long ago, in order to begin to live
in very truth the Kingdom of Heaven Way of Life here
and now on earth.

This was the burden of Aletheia's new message, and
it caused great consternation and bewilderment among
those who heard it. For who, her friends demanded,
could possibly begin to live that kind of life here and
now in this fallen world? Such an Ideal surely will only
be possible when we put off these mortal bodies and

reach the heavenly world, or when the glorious time comes for the Kingdom of Heaven to manifest itself on earth in some distant Golden Age.

But the Prince of Peace Himself came to earth two thousand years ago on purpose to reveal this great truth to us, answered Aletheia. He calls us to enter the Kingdom of Heaven now, and that means beginning to live now the kind of life which we know all will live when His Kingdom is established on earth. For how can that Kingdom possibly come on earth if no one is willing to begin demonstrating that glorious Way of Life, showing how unspeakably superior and blessed it is to the fallen Way of the World's life?

There was no response to the new, earnest appeal, only silence and withdrawal. Certainly there was no loud outcry against the message as there had been from Mountain Top City, but all the invitations to speak and teach ceased. Soon there were no openings at all for her to witness among any of the groups who had so eagerly welcomed the earlier messages. This new one was too difficult to accept, and no one wanted to hear it.

Zeal expressed the greatest consternation of all. "Aletheia," he expostulated, "this cannot possibly be right. So many people were being blest and helped by our witness, and they need your teaching about the Way of Holiness more and more. You are casting aside all your God-given opportunities to help needy people who are not yet sufficiently developed in their spiritual growth to be able to accept this higher teaching. So give it up for the time being, and accommodate your message to their need and to the level which they have reached. Give them what they are able to bear and not what they are not yet ready for. Did not our Lord Himself say, 'I have many things to say to you but you cannot hear them now.' Then follow His example and lay aside this higher teaching for the present."

"No," said Aletheia gently, but very firmly. "I cannot do that. There are many other splendid and inspired messengers who can give what these dear and beloved friends *can* accept and be helped by here in these blessed green pastures on the slopes of the High Places. They can fit and prepare their listeners and themselves to go higher when the time comes, and they are ready and able to do so. But I must not stay behind now that I have seen a higher Truth. I cannot unsee what I have seen. I cannot possibly go on sharing this way of life which wrongs the other living souls so deplorably and turns the whole Body of Creation into a groaning Creation, nailed to a cross of anguish. I cannot continue to 'crucify our Lord afresh' day by day by sharing in the fallen way of life. I cannot continue to put to death the image and likeness of God in the nature of Mankind, even in the nature of those who love Him and seek to do His will, but who have not yet seen this truth. I must press on to those yet more glorious High Places of Truth which I saw from the shining summits above these green slopes. I must go 'farther on and higher up' towards the true Homeland of my soul."

Zeal turned away silently, his head bowed upon his chest, and Aletheia started off alone once more—eastwards, towards the rising sun.

This time—although her heart ached with sorrow at the loss of all the happy fellowship that had been hers, and most of all at the absence of Zeal, whose support and companionship had always been such a very special joy—her heart was also filled with an enormous relief, with a sense of having been rescued from a great and terrible danger.

"Once on that terrible pinnacle seat," said Aletheia to herself with a shudder, "there would have been no escape. I would have lost once and for all the chance to see and respond to anything higher. Those who put me there would have held me a prisoner until I fell headlong from the pinnacle from utter exhaustion and strain, and someone else would be waiting to take the vacated seat! There must be many pinnacles which face eastwards where far more advanced souls than myself can be trusted to sit, and from which to teach great multitudes, but that pinnacle to which I was invited would have been my destruction. For the sake of such eminence I was in danger of losing my soul."

So she pressed on her journey eastward in response to the far summons from the still Higher Places. She had travelled only one day when she heard steps running behind her and a well-known and beloved voice called her name. Turning, she saw Zeal hastening towards her. A new Zeal, too—she could see that at first glance—shining with happiness and love, and a new, gentle humility which she had seen shining out of the faces of her own parents as a little child, though she had not known then what it was.

"Aletheia," he cried, as he came up to her. "Here I am! O forgive me that once again I let you start alone. But I, too, went up to the summit of the High Places and saw the vision. I know that it is true, and I, too, cannot unsee what I have seen. We will go together to the yet Higher Places of Truth and Goodness and of God's Love."

So they journeyed joyfully on and talked together of what they had seen. They lifted their hearts in communion with their Invisible Lord and they found that, like little children, they were learning more and more about the new Way of Life to which they had been called. They discovered still greater challenges and implications in the vision they had seen. Almost daily, they were shown new ways in which to practice the Holy Harmless Way of Life, and new aspects that they had never suspected.

Then one day they saw lovely green hills rising before them. In the dawn light, towering above those hills rose the beautiful snowy ranges towards which they were journeying. As they drew closer they found at the bottom of the hills a high wall which they could not climb, making it impossible for them to go any further.

However, the path led them directly up to a great closed gate on which they knocked. The gate swung a little ajar and there stood a great and glorious angel with a drawn sword in his hand which glittered in the light of the sun as though it were a naked flame of fire.

The angel looked at the two awestruck human beings standing at the gate and asked gently why they had knocked.

"We saw those shining high places above these hills from a long way off," answered Aletheia earnestly, "and we come seeking a way to reach them."

"The only way is through this gate," replied the angel, "but this is the gate of the Garden which the Lord God planted eastward in Eden [Gen. 2:8] in the dawn of the created world. Human beings were expelled long ago from this Paradise to wander in the wilderness of a fallen world. They cannot return here unless they see and love once again the Truth on which they turned their backs, and the Great and Glorious Commandment which they disobeyed and which caused their Fall. Do you two know the long lost Truth and the

Great Commandment upon which the whole life of this Paradise of Eden is based? For if not, I may not let you enter here."

"The lost Truth!" exclaimed Aletheia in a trembling voice, and her eyes were filled with tears. "The lost Truth which we have seen once again is that all creatures form one great Creation or Body into which the Creator Himself breathes His own Spirit and Life and consciousness, so that He Himself actually feels and experiences all that is done to, and is experienced by, every member in the Body. What we do to any living creature, great or small, we do also to Him, and He feels it, too."

The angel nodded and said gently, "That is well. And what is the one Great Commandment which rules in Eden?"

"The One Great Commandment," said Zeal earnestly, "we have been learning about on the way hither. It is the great, royal Law of Love. Since we now know the long lost Truth once again, we also know that we must love the Great Creator with all our heart, soul, mind, and strength. We must love and treat every living creature, without exception, as we want to be loved and treated ourselves. Not only does the Creator Himself feel it, but the great Law of Life is also that whatever we do to others in the One Body of Creation, we do also to ourselves. We must, in some way, at some time, experience in ourselves all that we have said and done. And so we knock on this door and ask to be allowed back into 'the Garden of the Lord' here in Eden, so that we may learn more fully about the perfect and glorious Ideal Way of Life from which Mankind fell so long ago, and may be allowed to ascend to the Shining Heights above."

Then the angel lifted his golden aureoled head and gave a happy, triumphant laugh and said, "Welcome back, little children, to your long-lost home." Then he bowed, and holding the gate wide open said, "Come inside. Everything here is yours to enjoy and to profit by, and there are teachers from those glorious Higher Places towering above these hills who will come down to teach you the things you need to know, understand, and practice before you can go up to those High Places you so long to reach. This is 'the Garden of the Lord,' where He put the Man whom he had made in His own image and likeness, and to whom He gave dominion over all the living creatures in the glorious Body of Creation. Come in that you may have restored to you everything which was lost by the Fall."

10
The
Garden of
Eden

Hand in hand Aletheia and Zeal went in through the gate, back into the Garden of Eden Way of Life to Mankind's long-lost home. They were awestruck and almost overcome with the joy and wonder of their privilege.

As they stepped in through the gate they saw stretching before them the peaceful green slopes of many hillsides. At the foot of those slopes there were the most beautiful gardens, orchards, and parklands that they had ever seen. Amongst the flowers fluttered brilliant-colored insects of every hue, busy about their own happy work of obtaining nectar and nourishment, as well as fertilizing the plants all over the gardens. Among the trees were multitudes of birds at their appointed work of keeping the trees clean and healthy by feeding on the mosses and lichens growing on their trunks, and at the right season, helping to scatter the seeds and fruits in the right places and thus ensure the new growth for the coming season. It was such happy work that they sang as they went about it from morning until night.

Little animals also scampered up and down the trees, busy with their own delightful occupations. Multitudes of others burrowed in the ground, making cozy homes for themselves amongst the roots of the trees and long tunnels of underground cities. In this way, they helped to aerate the subsoil, keeping it loose and fertile. Armies of ministering worms did the most important work of all—passing the soil through their bodies, enriching it and turning all the fallen leaves and grasses into richest loam and compost.

Herds of peaceful creatures cropped the grass, keeping it short and beautifully tended, and creatures of all kinds cooperated in doing everything which needed to be done without the help of spade, plow, or mower. Instinctively and happily they fulfilled the special functions which they had been created to perform in the glorious and wonderful "Economy of Nature."

As Aletheia and Zeal stood just inside the gate, looking at the beauty and perfection of the scene, they could see no adult human beings anywhere. Everywhere in the fields and gardens there were troops of merry, dancing, little children playing together and with the birds and beasts in the most innocent and gentle way. The creatures evidently rejoiced in their presence, some watching over them with the most careful vigilance and others scampering up the trees in order to throw down fruits and nuts for the little ones to eat. Some were even strewing soft grasses beneath special trees whose long, leaf-covered branches bent right over to the earth, making protective curtains for the children who evidently slept on grassy beds at night.

There was such innocent beauty and tender friendship between all the creatures and dwellers in the gardens that Aletheia and Zeal felt their hearts throbbing with a happy love and joy of a kind they had never felt before. Yet, it had something exquisitely familiar about it, as though at long last, after journeyings in sad, desert places, they had returned to their real home country.

At last they took a few steps forward into the garden. The birds, beasts, and little children saw them and hurried towards them with the most excited joy, astonishment, and delight, announcing the arrival to those further away by a variety of warbles, sounds, and happy laughter. Birds alighted on their shoulders. Animals rubbed joyfully against their legs. Little hands clutched excitedly at their hands and clothes. Aletheia and Zeal lifted the children in turn, and held them in their arms, and pressed them tenderly against their hearts. Each child looked up into their faces with love and astonished delight at being thus hugged and cherished. When set down so that the next little ones might have their turn, they immediately hurried to the end of the dancing, singing, and clapping queue, in order to experience yet again the new joyful feeling of being held in the arms of a father and mother for the first time.

What joy and excitement there was as the little ones joyfully led their new parents around the gardens, showing them all their favorite places—the quiet crystal-clear little pools where they bathed themselves and swam amongst the colorful, darting fish, the leafy curtained bedrooms, the soft green lawns and banks beneath special fruit and nut trees where the birds and squirrels brought them food and taught them to climb the branches for themselves.

The birds continually called the joyful news as they flew from tree to tree across the gardens of the arrival of two beautiful and loving big human beings. The animals all were entranced by their arrival and unwilling to spend a moment out of their presence except when scampering off to bring them a gift of something special to eat or to show the way to some enticing, new spot. It was evident that their arrival fulfilled some special need which all the inhabitants of the garden had felt, perhaps only subconsciously. Something which had been lacking was now plainly recognized as completing and perfecting the real heart's desire of every creature in the gardens. It was as though they had all been waiting for the manifestation of a perfect Ideal—

for the return of their first, lost parents into whose loving, gentle and wise care they had been committed in the beginning. Aletheia and Zeal realized, with a strange joy mingled with a yearning sorrow, that evidently in this part of the Garden, at least, they were the first adults to arrive back home to the place from which they had so long been missing. Their hearts trembled and exulted at the sweet and awesome wonder of it.

When the long, happy day drew to a close, they went to rest with the little ones under the trees. Once again they slept with the utter, peaceful innocence which Mankind lost so long ago, untroubled by any anxieties, regrets, or uneasy dreams of any kind.

When the new day broke and the sun's bright beams began to penetrate the leafy curtains of their rest room, they woke and found a packed circle of eager, loving little faces gazing at them rapturously while waiting to see how much longer it would be before they woke. Happy shouts of laughter and much clapping of little hands announced the exciting fact that the wonderful new father and mother were now awake. They eagerly escorted them once again to a place where "a river, clear as crystal" flowed through the garden, forming lovely cascades and shallow pools that invited them to the delight of a morning bath. Then they all ate breakfast on its green banks beneath the fruit trees which grew all along its edge.

Two or three happy and blissfully peaceful days passed. Then shining people from the snowy heights rising above Eden came down to the gardens and bade Aletheia and Zeal follow them up to the green slopes rising beyond the gardens. Here they were now privileged to be invited to learn new heavenly lessons.

The children, for the first time in their experience, felt regret and disappointment. But they were tenderly reassured that in the afternoon their new parents would return to them and spend the rest of the day and night with them. Furthermore, they would have lovely new things to tell them about and teach them; so the children watched them depart with many handwavings, kisses, and earnest little exhortations to "come back soon—quite soon." Then Aletheia and Zeal set off with their new teachers to the appointed place of learning.

In this book it is only possible to give a very brief outline of the wonderful lessons they learnt on the slopes above the earthly Paradise. In those blessed classrooms where they were then privileged to learn they were not by any means the only pupils. Others were there from many different earthly spheres and lands, but Aletheia and Zeal did not find a single pupil from their own part of the world. They entered with great joy into the new fellowship of those Higher Places and the lessons concerning the Ideal Life to which they were now returning.

11

The First Lesson in Eden:

The Blessed Laws of Paradise Life

This is just a brief outline of some of the lovely lessons which Aletheia and Zeal learned up on the green slopes above the Garden of Eden.

"You are now," began their teacher, "permitted to experience the earliest stages of the blessed Ideal Way of Life, which the wise and loving Creator meant all Mankind and all living creatures to experience."

They were to live in harmony with three beautiful and blessed Laws which were to govern their lives and cause only good and happy things to manifest themselves around them and in their own bodies. These laws would also ensure that every living soul had gloriously interesting and satisfying occupations so that they would never experience boredom and know how to pass their time happily. Every living creature in the Garden of Eden would not only be thankful to be alive, but would also grow and develop in the capacity to enjoy goodness in greater and greater measure. Thus, they would be able to rise to higher levels of God's truth and goodness. They would be entrusted with yet higher and more glorious forms of creative power as they learned how to use that power to the greatest benefit and advantage of all.

These three beautiful commands or principles governing the Way of Life in Paradise were taught to the man who was made in "the image and likeness of God" by the Creator Himself. The first of these principles was, "Be fruitful and multiply, replenish the earth, and subdue it"; namely, cause it to remain under the control of these laws so that nothing will be allowed to become out of harmony or contrary to the Ideal Will of the Creator (Gen. 1:28).

"Replenish the earth." This means to carry on the lovely work of the Creator, causing good and beautiful things to manifest and multiply under His guidance and instruction so that the world would continually be replenished.

Mankind in the Garden of Eden were to be fruitful themselves and teach this beautiful principle of creating goodness to their children and their children's children. Then they would be creators causing Goodness to manifest in increasing abundance throughout the whole universe.

In Eden they learned under the loving instruction of

the Lord and through their own experience that everything that is thought and desired will be expressed in some way; and that everything that is expressed in word or deed will then be manifest in visible forms or happenings. They learned the creative principles governing the thoughts and desires of the heart, guiding them in harmony with God's will so that only good would take form and add to the joy of all. They learned from the Creator Himself how to create the lovely things that He Himself had spoken into existence and how to act in order to experience and enjoy them. Just as God spoke everything into being on seven levels of consciousness, so too did they.

There is wonderful, secret wisdom hidden in the Book of Truth, ready to be revealed to those who can be trusted to use it in the right way, who have eyes to see, and hearts which long to know and understand. Such were the students in the classrooms where Aletheia and Zeal were then privileged to learn. As the Greatest Teacher of all said to His disciples, "Blessed are you for you see and hear things that have been hidden from the beginning of the world, which the wisest have longed to discover but could not, but they have been revealed unto babes and sucklings" (Matt. 11:25).

It was wonderful indeed for Aletheia and her fellow students to learn that every *instinctive* holy thought, desire, and action which they expressed in some way would later manifest itself in the form of a beautiful fish, a bird singing joyfully amongst the trees, or an exquisite insect helping to fertilize every flower it touched. Every holy physical desire and appetite they expressed through their bodily powers and faculties caused the wonderful diversities of the animal kingdom to manifest: the speed of the horse, the surefootedness of the antelope, the strength of the ox, the meekness of the sheep and lambs, the merry fun of the monkeys, the courage of the lion, and the devoted companionship of the dog. These were all visible forms of their own physical behavior and desires mirrored, as it were, before them in all these beautifully diverse animal forms that beautified and fertilized their Garden Home.

The use they made of their mental faculties caused wonderful material things to appear around them: buildings, cultivated gardens, orchards, and fields. But their moral desires and actions toward one another and toward all the living creatures created and controlled their relationships with each other, and made the Garden a beautiful home, full of loving and happy brothers and sisters seeking to add continually to the joy of everyone living there.

After learning to express goodness through their Paradise bodies, they would be ready to learn how to express still higher forms of goodness and beauty on the higher level of angelic God-consciousness. They would be entrusted with even higher powers and faculties than those they enjoyed in the Garden Home of Eden. After learning how to use the beautiful, creative instrument of an angelic body or holy personality, they would mature to the highest level of all—fully developed children of God, able to express the attributes of the Divine Nature in the most perfect forms of all, and to enjoy and experience goodness, beauty, and happiness on the divine level forever. This was the Creator's glorious destiny for all living creatures, as spirits learning to use the instruments of different bodies on ever-ascending higher levels of consciousness and power, creating glorious forms of goodness with which to populate all the shining stars and galaxies in the universe. Meanwhile, they were entrusted with Edenic bodies to use wisely and lovingly. Then when they had proved faithful in their present work they would be privileged, at the right time, to ascend to the next level of angelic life, experience, and creativity.

These beautiful secrets and principles of the Paradise life were taught to the first Mankind by the Lord Himself, as described in Genesis 2:19–20, where we read that the Lord brought all the living creatures to Adam so that he might give them names describing their special functions. He was to recognize also that each living creature was a reflection in visible form of some expressed desire and action of his own, manifesting on the appropriate level of his consciousness; and that he himself was conscious in those forms, sharing their experiences as his own emotions, physical satisfactions, and mental, moral and spiritual joys. Thus, he discovered the fruits and results of all that he had expressed and brought into being in exactly the same way as the Great Father Creator feels and experiences in all that He has brought into existence. In this way Man can learn how lovely it is only to express himself in beautiful and good ways and never be tempted to express any emotion or desire, which he would not be happy to experience himself.

The second wonderful principle which Man had to learn and live in harmony with, was revealed in the command in Genesis 1:28: "Have dominion over the fish of the sea and over the fowl of the air and over every living creature (or soul) that moveth upon the earth."

They were granted dominion over every living soul that God had brought into existence on earth, because they were to represent Him to all the other creatures. As they were "made in the image and likeness of God Himself," who is the Eternal Will to express goodness only, they were to exercise a dominion of wise love and goodness like His own, and to cause every living creature in the Garden to love, obey, and follow their directions just as they delighted to obey the will of God themselves and to revel in all His goodness and loving kindness. In their treatment of the other creatures, their tender care for them, and interest in all that they did, they were to mirror the love and kindness of God Himself. By exercising this loving, wise dominion over every living thing in the garden, treating them as they themselves loved and enjoyed being treated by God, they would find their highest happiness and satisfaction. They would feel the happiness of the creatures as their own happiness, and so their own lives would be increasingly enriched with the joy experienced in the myriads of forms under their loving dominion.

This second wonderful principle or law of the Garden of Eden Way of Life is summed up in these words: "To obey the Royal Law of Love and love and treat every creature as you want to be loved and treated yourself; that is, if you love your neighbor you will do well" (James 2:8, paraphrase).

Dominion over others can only be entrusted to those who will never abuse it, but will use it as an opportunity to mirror in their own conduct the divine loving kindness and goodness, and so to make those under their dominion thankfully joyful to be alive and free to perform their own special functions and work, and to develop in skill ever more perfectly until the time comes for them to be entrusted with a still more beautiful bodily instrument on the next level of God-consciousness.

The third principle or law of the Garden of Eden Way of Life concerned the food of all creatures. It was the injunction the Lord gave in Genesis 1:29-30: "And God said, behold, I give you every herb bearing seed, which is upon the face of all the earth, and every tree, in which is the fruit of a tree yielding seed; to you it shall be for meat. And to *every* beast of the earth, and to *every* fowl of the air, and to *everything* that creepeth upon the earth, wherein there is life, I have given every green herb for meat."

This was the great Food Law in Eden, God's expressed will and command that all living things should nourish themselves upon *the Plant Kingdom only*. Mankind, birds, beasts, and reptiles were to develop their strength and powers by feeding upon plants. Fruits, herbs, nuts, and cereals were to be their food; and all creatures at different levels of development had their own beautiful functions to perform in helping to maintain the harmonious economy of nature in the Garden by helping to produce the glorious varieties of plant foods suitable for each species of creature. The insects were to help fertilize the plants; the birds to scatter the seeds; the animals to manure the ground and keep the soil open to the air and light; human beings to sow, reap, plant, and harvest the fruits and vegetables and learn how to produce delicious and health-producing food.

Of course these three principles and commands were

"very good" indeed, but poor, poor human beings have completely forgotten them, and thereby have brought disease and death into the world, the most terrible sufferings of all kinds. The command that all living creatures should nourish their bodies upon the plant kingdom only meant that not a single creature in the Garden ever thought of attacking and preying upon any other creature, nor of using force in order to get what they desired. Never would any creature do anything so horrible as actually killing another living soul, depriving him of the glorious gift of life or of then eating their corpses as nourishment for their own bodies. Such a hideous practice was inconceivable in the Garden of Eden as it first was when the Creator had finished His glorious work and "saw everything that He had made, and, behold, it was very good."

The deplorable things fallen human beings now do outside Eden could not even be imagined, for every creature was an expression of goodness only. Therefore, no creature at that time had developed any form of defense mechanism with which to protect itself from its brothers in their beautiful Garden home. No living soul possessed fangs, poison stings, claws with which to scratch and tear, or talons or fierce beaks with which to rend flesh. Nothing in the way of a defense mechanism was needed, for all creatures were holy and harmless and nourished their bodies in the way their Creator had commanded, with wholesome strengthening food, and their minds with holy, happy knowledge appropriate to the level on which they were conscious. As a consequence, sickness, disease, death, and corruption of their bodies were unknown.

These were the three glorious principles about which Aletheia and the other students on the slopes above the Garden of Eden were taught, recovering in this way the first Ideal of the Perfect Way of Life which was the original design of the Great Creator. There was only One Negative Law in that Ideal Life: Thou shalt not.

12

The Tree of the Knowledge of Good and Evil

The command not to eat of one special tree in the Garden, the "tree of the knowledge of good and evil," was the only "Thou shalt not" known to the Garden of Eden Mankind. It was a test tree, put there to give Man the opportunity of resisting the temptation to do anything that was not good or that one would not like to have done to oneself. This expressed the will of the Creator of GOOD things only, that nothing *not* good must be mixed with the good, for that would produce evil or not-good consequences. If living souls began to do evil, they would eat or experience the not-good consequences in their bodies and in their surroundings, just as they experienced the blessed consequences of expressing goodness continually, and eating and enjoying its results.

Adam asked the Lord, his teacher, "What is *evil*, O Lord God? How can we recognize that it is not good?"

The answer was, "It is behaving to others in some way that you would not like them to behave to you, or doing something to yourself which it would not be right for you to do to others." You will recognize everything that is evil by the results which follow and are not good to experience. For example, an ignorant child may want to scramble over sharp rocks that might cut its feet or cause it to fall and suffer pain. That would be a form of evil. But if you, as a wise parent, lovingly teach your children what it will not be good for them to do, and explain to them that the results which would follow would not be good or happy to experience, then they will be warned and will not hurt themselves or others. If, however, one of the children decides that he is big enough and wise enough to be able to climb those rocks without falling, and chooses to do so in spite of your warning and falls and gets hurt, that is not just evil but SIN, too.

EVIL is everything which produces bad consequences, but if it is done ignorantly there is no blame or condemnation attached to it. The child learns, through the consequences, not to repeat this action. But a loving warning and commandment wilfully rejected is sinful, especially if the choice caused evil results to others, though advantageous to oneself. Then the SINNER discovers the Great Law in the universe which decrees that the sinner must himself suffer in some way the consequences of his sin and must atone for any evil experiences he inflicts upon others. All suffering is atoning as a result of doing things which cause evil results. The suffering teaches wisdom. It helps to deter one from repeating the same mistake ignorantly; God uses the sinner's suffering as reparation for the harm done to others.

The temptation presented to Mankind in Eden was to do something that they had been forbidden to do, such as breaking one or the other of the three laws governing the Garden of Eden Way of Life—the original Ideal of God for all Mankind. However, the wise and loving warning not to mix any evil with the good was disobeyed. Mankind began to treat the other living creatures under their dominion, in ways they would not want to be treated themselves. Then they did evil things to human beings, too; and the beautiful, perfectly good life in the Garden of Eden came to what seemed to be a disastrous end. Mankind fell from God-consciousness and awareness of goodness only into self-consciousness and awareness of evil in the most frightful and agonizing forms. As a result, the whole Creation has become "a groaning Creation" (Rom. 8:22), nailed to a cross of suffering. All sufferings are rooted in the breaking of this primeval law: "Thou shalt not eat of the tree of the knowledge of good and evil" (Gen. 2:17).

All that has happened since that catastrophic fall in

the long history of Mankind is the history of Man's descent into the abyss of evil and sin, and of the continual operation of God's grace and tender forgiving love in seeking to restore all fallen souls to their lost ideal life. Everything in the glorious Book of Truth is an account of fallen Mankind learning to loathe sin—either through suffering the consequences of evildoing, or through joyful communion with God and learning to express His will to goodness only. This is the glorious salvation of which the Bible speaks: full restoration to the glorious ideal from which Man fell—the life of Man made "in the image and likeness of God" (Gen. 1:27).

These are the two ways back to "the Father's House." First is the Way of Holiness, which is consecration to expressing goodness only, experiencing only good and beautiful results with no sorrow or suffering from evil things added. This way leads to the Mount of Transfiguration or of translation without passing through disease and death—like Enoch, who "walked with God: and he was not; for God took him" (Gen. 5:24). Second is atoning for evil and sin by suffering on the cross to which the whole fallen Creation is nailed; and to experience there the pains of a hell or purgatory, until every bit of desire for self-will and for anything not good is burnt out of the soul forever. When that has been accomplished, every purged soul will be resurrected to the glorious Ideal life once again in the resurrection Body rising from the cross.

These are the two ways of restoration to the Ideal Life, which were shown to Mankind in the glorious and awesome revelation made by Jesus in His life of perfect Holiness that expressed only goodness under every terrible test and situation. At the Mount of Transfiguration he received the power to bypass death completely, opening for Him a way back into the perfect Ideal Life which was God's original pattern for all Mankind, with power to rise or ascend higher and higher through the angelic level of God consciousness right back to the fully matured Son of God consciousness which is the glorious goal for all of us.

Having demonstrated that way of Holiness so perfectly and shown that it leads to transfiguration of the Body and not to death, He then voluntarily acquiesced in the Father's will that He should demonstrate the second way of atoning suffering—voluntarily, because there had been nothing in His life for which He needed to atone. But it was necessary that Mankind should see the Second Way revealed, too. If the Way of Holiness is not followed, but evil is mixed with good, until it seems that only evil is left and no good remains, then the purging of atonement must take place.

Thus, Jesus voluntarily allowed Himself to be nailed to the cross of suffering along with two thieves and murderers. His death revealed in awesome clarity the principle that if men sin, the way back to the Father's House can only be by a cross of purging and atoning sufferings. When that suffering has accomplished its purpose and purged every last drop of self-will from the soul, then there is a glorious resurrection—participation forever in the glorious Ideal Life which is God's plan and purpose for every living soul, an abundant entry into THE KINGDOM OF HEAVEN WAY OF LIFE, the kind of life which Jesus lived and demonstrated so perfectly under all circumstances while He was still living here in this fallen world. Salvation will be complete when mankind lives once again according to those three glorious Garden of Eden laws—replenishing the earth with goodness only, exercising a dominion of wise love over other living creatures, and nourishing themselves on the plant kingdom only so that nothing will hurt, destroy, or work evil to any other creature.

"Then the wolf also will dwell with the lamb, and the leopard shall lie down with the kid; and the calf and the young lion and the fatling together; and a little child shall lead them. And the cow and the bear shall feed; their young ones shall lie down together; and the lion shall eat straw like the ox. The suckling child shall play on the hole of the asp, and the weaned child shall put his hand on the scorpion's den. They shall not hurt nor destroy in all My *Holy Mountain* (the Highest level of

God-consciousness): for the earth shall be full of the Knowledge of the Lord, as the waters cover the sea" (Isa. 11:6–9).

Alas, for ages the followers of Jesus have crucified the blessed, holy, harmless way of the Lamb of God revealed by their Lord. They have remained blind to the truth revealed by His birth in a stable amongst the innocent, harmless birds and beasts—that He represented them just as He represents all the sons of men. Did He not twice cleanse the temple and liberate all the animal and bird victims gathered there which were to be slaughtered for the worshippers? Did not Jesus declare that such religious ideas and customs had changed the House of God into a den of thieves—where men become like wild beasts, slaughtering and feeding upon other living creatures? Did He not drive out the money changers who made their living by sharing in this evil custom of living at the expense of the sufferings and death of the "living souls" bought and sold for slaughter in the temple courtyard itself? Was He not Himself "the Lamb of God," who atoned for the sins of the world against the myriads of slaughtered and tortured birds and beasts whom the Creator had entrusted to the loving care of Mankind? Finally, on "The Table of the Lord," where His lovers and followers meet to remember His death, is there not to be found only harmless food taken from the plant kingdom alone—the bread and the juice reminding us of our lost Paradise Way of Life to which our Lord, by His own grace and suffering, is seeking to help us to return?

Surely it behooves all who love Him and who look longingly for "His return in full power and glory" to begin living according to that glorious Ideal now, so that they will not be ashamed at His coming, nor hear His sorrowful reply when they cry out: "Lord, Lord, have we not prophesied in Thy Name? and in Thy Name have cast out devils? and in Thy Name have done many wonderful works? Then I will profess unto you, I never knew you: depart from Me, ye that work iniquity" (Matt. 7:22–23). Instead of being able to follow Him to the Mount of Transfiguration or rapture and translation, they will have to share in the sufferings of the judgments that we bring upon ourselves when we wrong other creatures.

This, in brief, is a summary of the wonderful and glorious things taught by the Paradise teachers on the green slopes above the Garden of Eden.

13
The
Eagles'
Wings

The happy days (years, measured by earth time) slipped past while Aletheia and Zeal and the other students learned wonderful lessons on how to live once again the Ideal Life of Eden from which poor Mankind fell so long ago and had been searching to rediscover ever since.

As the days passed, the little innocent children in the Garden were led, one by one, or in twos and threes, by the angels out of that realm of complete innocence on to the pathway of earthly life, that they too might be able to learn holy lessons and grow and develop in goodness. They would always carry with them in the depths of their hearts the memory of their beautiful early home like treasure locked away in a casket, forgotten for a while until the right moment should come for the memories to be revived, awakening in them longings to start on the long, blessed journey homewards to the High Places, just as Aletheia had done.

Then one day the eastern gate of Eden, which was guarded by the great archangel, opened once again. Two more happy beings entered the garden hand in hand and were greeted by the children with all the same ecstasies of joy that they had lavished upon Aletheia and Zeal. For them too it was a very special joy to welcome the newcomers; for they were the first fruits of the witness which they had given on the last High Places which they had left behind when they renounced the rocky throne of acclaim and popularity, in order to be free to seek the still higher things.

What a blessed and happy reunion it was, but fraught also with great significance for Aletheia and Zeal. For when they led the two newcomers to the classroom on the higher slopes above Eden, their heavenly teacher looked lovingly at them, and then told Aletheia and Zeal that their course of lessons in that schoolroom was now to come to an end. New parents had entered Eden to care for the little ones who were still waiting to be led to the western gateway leading into earth life. Now it was time for them to take the next step and to ascend to the summit of the shining peaks above Eden, and from there they would see what they were to do next.

Aletheia and Zeal made loving farewells and tenderly entrusted the little ones to the care of the new parents. Then they set forth on their journey to the shining peaks above, joyfully and exultantly leaping up the mountainside on their "hinds' feet," full of blissful anticipation about what they would behold from the heights above the classrooms of Eden.

When they came to the top, they looked eastward, caught their breath and together broke into a shout of wonder and joy, and fell upon their knees to worship.

In the distance, far above the range on which they were standing, there towered heavenwards yet another range of silvery peaks, more glorious and wonderful than any they had seen before. They seemed to reach right up into the highest heavenly realms of all. As they gazed, awestruck and with passionate longing, their eyes were wonderfully sharpened and strengthened so that they could clearly see a glorious city, shining like the sun and situated upon the highest peak of all—the heavenly Mount Zion. Its gates were open, its pavements gleamed like gold, and multitudes of white-robed, heavenly people and shining angels were walking there or passing along the highways of the mountain range.

Both Aletheia and Zeal knew without a shadow of doubt that at last they were looking at their Home—the real Home toward which they had been steadfastly making their way. This was the Father's House, the goal of their long pilgrimage, the place of their hearts' deepest desires and longings, "the city not made with hands, whose Builder and Maker is God Himself."

A broad plain stretched before them below the peak on which they were standing. Taking one another's hands, the two of them leaped and ran, almost as though on winged feet, across the plain and towards the shining, Heavenly world beckoning to them from afar.

Swiftly and easily they reached the farther side of the plain where they expected to begin the ascent to those stupendous heights towering into the Heavens above. But they were brought to a standstill just in the nick of time, for they suddenly discovered that the plain ended on the brink of a vast abyss which stretched left and right unendingly—an abyss so broad and deep that it seemed as though the whole solar system might have been plunged into it and have been swallowed up completely.

There they were, on the brink of an apparently bottomless abyss that stretched between them and the Homeland for which they had been seeking for so long with no possible way to cross it.

They stood there while Aletheia gave a little, gasping sob and cried out, "Oh, what must we do? There, high above and completely unreachable, is our true Homeland, and it seems there is no possible way by which we can reach it!" Then she burst into heartbroken tears and sank back to the ground.

"Be of good courage," whispered Zeal comfortingly.

"There must be a way or we would not have been guided here. Perhaps somewhere there is a path down into the abyss. Let us look."

Aletheia gave another little sobbing cry of terror, "Oh, no, no, no!" she gasped. "Even with hinds' feet we could never go down such a bottomless precipice as that! Supposing it really is bottomless?"

Zeal stooped and picked up a piece of rock and threw it over the edge, down into the abyss. They waited and waited to hear it land on some firm bottom far below, or with a splash into water, but there was no sound at all. They looked left and right. A path ran all along the edge of the abyss in both directions, but with no end in sight, even though their eyes were now able to see to the end of the earth.

Zeal stood there supporting Aletheia, who was crouching, weeping, on the ground. In the awestruck silence which filled his heart a sound became audible, rising up from the vastness of the abyss—a burst of pitiful moans and groans, distant shouts and screams, and sounds of indescribable anguish, as though hell with all its horror and despairing woe had opened at their feet.

Zeal stooped down, lifted Aletheia, and, supporting her with his arms, said gently, "Aletheia, all that we have been learning on our journey through the years as we travelled to the higher and yet higher places has led us to this. Here we are within view of the Highest of All. Let us look up there and rejoice that, shining above us is the goal that we have been seeking for so long. Let us ask together for help to be given us and guidance as to how we are to arrive at the final goal."

Aletheia opened her eyes, looked and again burst into a little cry of joy and rapture. There, on the other side of the abyss, far above, *were* the Highest Places of All. She recognized them and knew that they were indeed the Homeland of her soul to which she was returning after long wanderings—returning Home to be welcomed by "the Father of all Spirits" (Heb. 12:9), after her long term at School. All the time the memory of her Home before she started on her earthly lives had been deeply engraved. She now realized that she had never been absolutely free from the pangs of homesickness and yearning to return to the Father's House.

Then she heard Zeal calling across the abyss, up to the shining multitudes on the Heavenly slopes above them.

"Send forth Thy light and Thy Truth, let them lead us; and bring us to Thy Holy Hill (Ps. 43:3). Father in Heaven, show us what to do."

Then one of the shining ones up there in the Heavenly World spread white pinions and winged his way to them across the yawning abyss. He stood beside them, smiling with Heavenly joy, love, and reassurance.

"Fear not," he said. "You are nearly at the end of your journey, so be of good cheer, and press forward on your way."

"But how?" faltered Aletheia, and looked at him pleadingly. "How can we go forward, for this terrible abyss stretches before us. Is there a pathway somewhere, leading down into it and up the other side?"

"No, there is no pathway anywhere."

"Then where does this pathway along the edge of the abyss lead to?"

"Only to Death and back again to the earth from which you are now returning Home."

"Then how can we go forward and upwards if we have no wings like you? We cannot fly across it. Can you carry us in your arms?"

He smiled and shook his head. "No," he said. "There is only one way to reach the Highest, and that is by being willing to go down into the lowest and learn to feel with those who have fallen to the lowest depths of all. Aletheia and Zeal, you must leap down into the abyss if you want to mount up to the Highest of All. It is the only way to get there."

"Leap into the abyss? We shall be dashed to pieces!"

"There is no other way to the Highest but by going down into the lowest, to seek to succour and rescue those who have fallen into the depths of the lowest hells. Just as the Highest of All showed when He came to earth."

Aletheia and Zeal stood for a few moments in stunned silence. Aletheia began to shake from head to foot and would have fallen if Zeal had not been supporting her. For long moments neither of them spoke, but in the deathlike silence sounds rose again from the depths of the abyss like a far-off sea moaning on to a shore of lonely, despairing suffering.

At last Zeal spoke. "There, shining above us, is our Homeland," he said. "Were we not led to leave it, long, long ago, just so that we might learn how to return to it, enriched by all our experiences in the School of Earth existence? If there is no way back to it except through the abyss of the lowest, then that is the way that we must go, and we shall be given grace to do so. For never yet has the enabling grace failed to be granted. Of course, it is the way our Lord Himself went, Aletheia. Should we not follow the same way, also? Even if we are dashed to pieces it will be only our bodies that perish, and we shall be raised up from death as He was. Come, Aletheia, let us leap down together into the abyss, and let us do it rejoicingly."

Aletheia looked at him with wonder and comfort, for now it was Zeal, who had lagged behind at other times, who was the first to understand and respond to

the Highest Truth of all—that there is no way to the joy
of the Highest Heaven except by willingness to go
down to succour those in the lowest Hell. She put her
hand in his and said, "Yes, we will leap down together;
we are perfectly safe in our Father's love."

"The Angel of His Presence" gave a laugh of happy,
radiant joy. "I will go with you," He said, and taking
Aletheia's other hand in His, He made a sign and the
three of them leaped down together into the abyss.

For one dizzy moment it seemed as though they were
falling; and then, wonder of wonders, both Zeal and
Aletheia felt great and powerful pinions unfolding
around them, bearing them gently lower and lower into
the darkness below. Down they floated as smoothly
and easily as the eagles wheel down from their mountain eyries to the valleys far below. Presently their feet
touched solid ground and they realized that they had
made the seemingly impossible descent with perfect
ease and safety. They folded their wings and looked
about them.

14

The
Highest
Heaven

They found themselves in a place of terrible darkness, but from their own bodies there glimmered a soft and penetrating light which enabled them to see quite a distance in every direction. They were standing on a vast plain which was covered with rocks, briars, and thorn trees; and there were companies of people stumbling amongst the rocks and tearing themselves upon the thorns, all the time uttering cries of pain, fear, and woe.

As they stood there peering about them, someone suddenly stumbled against Aletheia. She put out her arms to support a falling body and cried out in warning, "Oh, take care! Do let me help you. There are so many sharp rocks and bushes around here and I can see them, while perhaps you, in the dark, cannot."

But the person who had tripped against her began kicking violently and beating the air with his hands, shouting, "Let me go! Don't dare to attack me! I'll kill you if you do!"

The blows seemed to fall upon her quite harmlessly and painlessly, and as gently as possible, she assured him that she was a friend and only wanted to help in any way she could. But the man broke away from her and immediately stumbled against a rock and fell to the ground, where he lay groaning pitiably.

Aletheia was deeply distressed by what had happened, but almost at once another person stumbled into her, and she could hear Zeal trying to help someone else. This time it was a woman who fell against Aletheia, and to her horror and bewilderment the same thing happened again. The moment the woman fell, she began to beat at Aletheia with her hands, shrieking as though in deadly fear. Aletheia's loving words were unable to reassure her. The woman, too, broke away and soon there were cries of pain and the sound of tearing rags as she became entangled in the branches of a cruel thorn tree.

Again and again the same thing happened. Aletheia and Zeal's distress for the poor people thus stumbling and suffering in the darkness increased all the time until they could hardly bear it. Whenever they tried to help those within reach or who stumbled against them, each person at once reacted as though an enemy were attacking them.

At last the terrible truth dawned upon them. With a shock of horror they realized that all the people around them were both blind and deaf. They could neither hear what was said nor perceive the proffered hands. To them every person they stumbled against in the utter darkness and deathly silence was an enemy to be feared and fled from.

As this realization dawned upon Aletheia and Zeal, dismay filled their hearts. What could be done for these people? They could neither hear nor see that friends were there longing to help them, so there was no way of persuading them to accept help or making them understand.

Just then a man's voice was heard shouting loudly and earnestly high above them. Evidently, he was standing on the edge of the abyss of blind and deaf souls, just as they had stood before they had leaped down into it; and his voice came ringing down the canyonlike walls, echoing and re-echoing in every direction. These were the words he was shouting with earnest warning and appeal.

"Cry aloud, spare not, lift up thy *voice* like a trumpet, and *show* My people their transgression and sin" (Isa. 58:1).

As they listened, the hearts of Aletheia and Zeal felt like lead within them. When his voice ceased for a moment, Zeal shouted up to him sorrowfully, "Oh! you don't understand! just as we didn't. It is no good crying ever so loudly, for all the souls down here are deaf; and even if you lift up your voice like a trumpet, they will not be able to hear you. And it's no use trying to *show* them their transgression and sin, for they are all blind and cannot see anything. Oh! may God help us! What *can* we do for them?"

The voice of the man at the top of the abyss was silent. Then with a surge of unspeakable relief and joy Aletheia and Zeal perceived that the Angel of the Lord's Presence was still standing beside them. He said: "I will tell you the one and only way in which you can help the blind and deaf to understand that you are a friend and want to help them."

He stooped and whispered the secret in their ears, and after hearing it, they stood there waiting, full of joyful expectation and hope.

Presently someone else stumbled against Aletheia, and she put out her arms and caught the falling body. Once again the poor blind-and-deaf soul reacted in the same way, raining blows and trying to escape from the loving grasp. But Aletheia tightened her hold and drew the struggling form right up against her heart. Then, very gently, she kissed first one cheek and then the other of the suffering one.

It was like a wonderful miracle—indeed it *was* a Heavenly miracle. For the poor, resisting soul instantly ceased struggling to escape and, instead, clung to Aletheia desperately. With heartbroken relief and longing, he sobbed, "Oh! are you someone who really loves me? Even here in this terrible darkness, loneliness, and silence? I beseech you not to leave me. Let me stay with you and feel the comfort of your presence. Oh! don't go away and leave me alone again, lost forever in this awful place."

Kissing the bleeding, tear-stained cheeks again, Aletheia began to lead the poor soul to where she saw, in the distance, a glimmer of dawnlight. Zeal followed with another poor soul, who clung to him and sobbed tremblingly, "Oh, don't go away and leave me. If you love me, stay with me and don't leave me alone in this awful torment."

So they went together until they came to a great and glorious waterfall pouring itself over the lip of the abyss from far above.

As soon as the spray from the fall fell on the faces of the poor, suffering souls, the blind eyes opened and the deaf ears unstopped. Suddenly all four of them found themselves looking into the most beautiful and wonderful face in the universe—the face of Holy, Forgiving Love Himself.

He put out His arms and drew the rescued souls to His heart. At that moment the whole terrible abyss vanished, and lo! they were all standing in the midst of

Heaven, in the city of Mount Zion itself, on the shining peaks on the other side of the abyss which it had seemed so impossible ever to reach. They were back Home in the Father's House and joining in the inexpressible joy of Heaven over souls rescued from the lowest places of all! They were all surrounded by an innumerable company of ministering spirits and holy angels, all of whom were also leading rescued souls into the Presence of Christ the Lord. They came up from the great abyss and sang with such joy, tenderness, and rapture that the whole universe seemed full of song.

Then they realized the overwhelming Truth: that even Hell itself is in the midst of Heaven, in the World of Light and Love, and it is only shut eyes and closed ears which cannot perceive the glorious fact that "in God we all live and move and have our being." In Him there is no darkness at all, nothing but love and goodness. Anything which seems not good is simply the nightmare dreams of those who have closed their eyes to the light, their ears to love, and so create their own unspeakably dreadful sorrows and woes until they are helped to open their eyes and ears once again, and to leave the dreadful world of self's false dreams for the real World of God's Presence and Joy.

The Highest Heaven of all is to find oneself incorporated into the Body of the Redeemer, as a living member in it with His authority to transmit His redemptive power to those who stumble in the darkness, silence, and terror of their self-created worlds—to help them to become conscious once again of the reality of Heaven all round about them. " 'Comfort ye, comfort ye My people,' saith the Lord. 'Speak comfortably to them,' " for only so can the blind and deaf in the depths of hell understand.

Aletheia and Zeal found themselves at the center of their hearts' desire and surrounded by a great company of welcoming friends and loved ones. There were Grace-and-Glory and Fearless Witness, the parents of Aletheia, and all the dear friends of her childhood. With what joy and love they were welcomed into the Courts of Heaven with the long, long journey now finished, and the Truth itself shining around them in inexpressible glory. Now it was their glorious privilege to go with all their loved ones into the abyss and share in the Highest rapture of all of being able to open the hells and lead souls up into Heaven.

Aletheia looked into the faces of her parents and cried with wondering joy, "Surely at last this must be the Highest Truth of all and the Highest Heaven with nothing beyond!" But they laughed with heavenly joy and answered, "Oh no, Aletheia. This is not the Highest, for don't you yet realize that God is an infinite, endless, boundless universe of goodness, ever rising to loftier heights and more glorious powers, privileges, and blessings? There is no end to the goodness and truth of the Eternal Loving Will to bring into existence nothing but goodness only.

"For the present this is the Highest Heaven for all of us, sharing with the holy angels and the Lamb in the heavenly joy of bringing souls up out of their hells into the heavenly places and restoration to the Father's House. But when the last soul has been rescued from the abyss of the blind and deaf, the last hell has been opened, and all *are* safely back in the Father's House with not one missing, then this Heaven will come to an end, for it will be needed no longer. Then there will be 'a new Heaven and earth,' infinitely more glorious even than this one, though we cannot at this stage possibly conceive of any joy greater than this nor any Heaven more perfect and glorious. Nevertheless, still higher and more glorious things do lie ahead, for it is written, 'Eye hath not seen, nor ear heard, neither have entered into the heart of man, the things which God hath prepared for them that love Him' " (1 Cor. 2:9).

So Aletheia and Zeal "entered into the joy of their Lord," into the Highest Heaven that we can conceive of at this stage. Shall we not press on towards the Highest that we are capable of seeing, until we, too, come, by the infinite grace and love of God, to the place where we are permitted to stand with the Lamb and the Holy Angels with authority and power to open the hells into which fallen souls have locked themselves and lead them up and back to the Father's House? That we, too, may experience the glorious life described in Hebrews 12:22–24: "Ye are come unto Mount Zion, and unto the City of the Living God, the heavenly Jerusalem, and to an innumerable company of angels. To the General Assembly and Church of the Firstborn, which are written in Heaven, and to God the Judge of all, and to the spirits of just men made perfect, and to Jesus the mediator of the better covenant."

Come! Let us press on to the Highest!